HAUNTING WITH THE STARS

GOOSEBUMPS®
HALL OF HORRORS

#1 CLAWS!
#2 NIGHT OF THE GIANT EVERYTHING
#3 SPECIAL EDITION: THE FIVE MASKS OF DR. SCREEM
#4 WHY I QUIT ZOMBIE SCHOOL
#5 DON'T SCREAM!
#6 THE BIRTHDAY PARTY OF NO RETURN

GOOSEBUMPS®
MOST WANTED

#1 PLANET OF THE LAWN GNOMES
#2 SON OF SLAPPY
#3 HOW I MET MY MONSTER
#4 FRANKENSTEIN'S DOG
#5 DR. MANIAC WILL SEE YOU NOW
#6 CREATURE TEACHER: FINAL EXAM
#7 A NIGHTMARE ON CLOWN STREET
#8 NIGHT OF THE PUPPET PEOPLE
#9 HERE COMES THE SHAGGEDY
#10 THE LIZARD OF OZ

SPECIAL EDITION #1 ZOMBIE HALLOWEEN
SPECIAL EDITION #2 THE 12 SCREAMS OF CHRISTMAS
SPECIAL EDITION #3 TRICK OR TRAP
SPECIAL EDITION #4 THE HAUNTER

GOOSEBUMPS®
SLAPPYWORLD

#1 SLAPPY BIRTHDAY TO YOU
#2 ATTACK OF THE JACK!
#3 I AM SLAPPY'S EVIL TWIN
#4 PLEASE DO NOT FEED THE WEIRDO
#5 ESCAPE FROM SHUDDER MANSION
#6 THE GHOST OF SLAPPY
#7 IT'S ALIVE! IT'S ALIVE!
#8 THE DUMMY MEETS THE MUMMY!
#9 REVENGE OF THE INVISIBLE BOY
#10 DIARY OF A DUMMY
#11 THEY CALL ME THE NIGHT HOWLER!
#12 MY FRIEND SLAPPY
#13 MONSTER BLOOD IS BACK
#14 FIFTH-GRADE ZOMBIES
#15 JUDY AND THE BEAST
#16 SLAPPY IN DREAMLAND

GOOSEBUMPS®

Also available as ebooks

NIGHT OF THE LIVING DUMMY
DEEP TROUBLE
MONSTER BLOOD
THE HAUNTED MASK
ONE DAY AT HORRORLAND
THE CURSE OF THE MUMMY'S TOMB
BE CAREFUL WHAT YOU WISH FOR
SAY CHEESE AND DIE!
THE HORROR AT CAMP JELLYJAM
HOW I GOT MY SHRUNKEN HEAD
THE WEREWOLF OF FEVER SWAMP
A NIGHT IN TERROR TOWER
WELCOME TO DEAD HOUSE
WELCOME TO CAMP NIGHTMARE
GHOST BEACH
THE SCARECROW WALKS AT MIDNIGHT
YOU CAN'T SCARE ME!
RETURN OF THE MUMMY
REVENGE OF THE LAWN GNOMES
PHANTOM OF THE AUDITORIUM
VAMPIRE BREATH
STAY OUT OF THE BASEMENT
A SHOCKER ON SHOCK STREET
LET'S GET INVISIBLE!
NIGHT OF THE LIVING DUMMY 2
NIGHT OF THE LIVING DUMMY 3
THE ABOMINABLE SNOWMAN OF PASADENA
THE BLOB THAT ATE EVERYONE
THE GHOST NEXT DOOR
THE HAUNTED CAR
ATTACK OF THE GRAVEYARD GHOULS
PLEASE DON'T FEED THE VAMPIRE
THE HEADLESS GHOST
THE HAUNTED MASK 2
BRIDE OF THE LIVING DUMMY
ATTACK OF THE JACK-O'-LANTERNS

ALSO AVAILABLE:
IT CAME FROM OHIO!: MY LIFE AS A WRITER by R.L. Stine

HAUNTING WITH THE STARS

R.L. STINE

SCHOLASTIC INC.

Goosebumps book series created by Parachute Press, Inc.
Copyright © 2022 by Scholastic Inc.

ISBN 978-1-338-75218-2

10 9 8 7 6 5 4 3 2 1   22 23 24 25 26

Printed in the U.S.A.   40
First printing 2022

SLAPPY HERE, EVERYONE.

Welcome to *SlappyWorld*.

Yes, it's Slappy's world. You're only *screaming* in it!

Did you miss me? I'm so wonderful, sometimes I miss *myself*! Hahaha.

I wish there were two of me so someone else could tell me how *amazing* I am!

I would call myself an awesome genius. But, you know, someone as brilliant and perfect as I am doesn't like to brag. Haha.

Some people think I'm evil. But they don't know me. If they did, they'd know that I'm *perfectly* evil! Hahaha.

I say give me a break. What's evil about wanting to scare everyone to death? We all need a hobby, right?

Our story today is about a boy named Murphy and his two friends Orly and Cleo. Murphy's hobby is outer space. He can't stop thinking about the stars, the planets, and the universe. Murphy's big wish is to be an astronaut and travel to other planets.

But, you know, sometimes getting your wish can be scary. Especially in one of MY stories! Hahaha!

I call this story *Haunting with the Stars*!

Go ahead. Start screaming. It's another one of my frightening tales from *SlappyWorld*.

MARS, HERE I COME

By Murphy Shannon

My parents know that I think and dream about the planets and stars and outer space all the time. That's why they took me to the headquarters of the US Spaceship Academy for my birthday.

I was so excited, I couldn't sit still in the backseat of our car. I kept bumping up and down. I could barely breathe. This was the best birthday present ever!

But I didn't know how outstanding it would be.

I would love to work for the Spaceship Academy when I grow up. I know it's a wild dream. But maybe I could even be an astronaut and travel to another planet or circle the stars.

My friends Orly and Cleo think I'm weird. And maybe I am. But can you think of anything more exciting than being a space pioneer?

When we arrived at Spaceship Academy head-quarters, I leaped out of the car before Dad even finished parking. I stared up at the huge shiny building and cried out, "Wow!" The building reached up to the sky. It was all glass and shaped like a giant rocket ship.

Of course I'd seen videos about this place. But it didn't look this awesome on a screen. The building looked like it could blast off to space by itself!

Dad showed his special pass, and a guard in a uniform covered in shiny medals pressed some numbers on a keypad. The doors slid open for us. We stepped into an entry hall that had to be a mile long!

I felt dizzy staring at the models of spaceships that lined the center of the hall. Big posters of astronauts and photos from the moon and Mars covered the walls.

I wanted to stop and study each model spacecraft. But Mom said we had an appointment with an Academy captain, and we couldn't be late.

A Spaceship Academy captain! Whoa. Could this birthday get any more awesome?

We stopped in front of a glass office door. The name CAPTAIN FARRELL DODGE was stenciled in black letters on the door.

"Go in, Murphy," Dad said. "The appointment is only for you."

My hand was shaking as I pushed open the door and stepped inside. The office walls were covered with charts and maps of the galaxy.

Captain Dodge sat behind a big metal desk. He also had medals up and down his uniform jacket. A model of a spaceship stood on one corner of his desk.

He stood up and smiled as I entered. He was pretty young. Much younger than my parents, I think. "Hello, Murphy," he said. "I've been waiting to meet you." He stepped around the desk and shook my hand.

"Th-thank you," I stammered. I was too excited to say anything else.

I sat down in the chair across from his desk. He took his seat and leaned forward to talk to me. "Your parents wanted you to have a birthday surprise," he said, speaking in a low voice. "But they don't know the real reason I agreed to your visit."

I blinked. "Excuse me? The real reason?"

He nodded. "This is top secret, Murphy. The Spaceship Academy doesn't want to start a panic." His voice was just above a whisper.

"I—I don't understand," I replied.

"It's the Martians," he said. "We've heard rumors. Rumors they plan to attack."

"Huh? Martians?" I said.

He nodded again. "That's why we need you. We need you to go on a secret mission to Mars. We need you to find out if the rumors are true."

"But—but—I'm just a kid!" I cried. "I'm only twelve."

"Yes. That's why we need you," he said. "The Martians will expect someone from the military. But they'll never expect a kid."

I stared at him. My brain was spinning. "Are you serious?" I asked in a tiny voice.

He leaned closer over the desk and whispered, "Murphy, we need you to leave immediately. Will you do it?"

I finished reading my story and turned to Mom. "What do you think? Do you like it?"

Mom smiled. "I like it a lot, Murphy," she said.

"It's a very good start to a story. You are such a good writer. You take after me. I took creative writing in college."

"I think it's the best thing I've ever written," I said. "I can't wait to show it to Mr. Hawkins." I waved the story pages in my hand. "But I have one problem with it . . ."

"What's that?" Mom asked.

"There's no ending," I said. "It just stops."

"Yes. I was wondering about that," Mom said. "What happens next? Does Murphy go to Mars?"

I shrugged. "I don't know," I said. "I can't decide what happens next. I'm totally stumped."

Mom thought about it for a moment. "Well, tomorrow is your school trip to the Rayburne Observatory," she said. "You'll be looking at Mars and all the planets and stars in the big telescope. I'll bet that will give you some ideas for your story."

Mom wasn't always right. But she was right about that. My trip to the observatory gave me *lots* of ideas. *Terrifying* ideas.

Orly Roberts laughed and punched me in the leg. "Murphy, you're so excited, you can't breathe!" she said.

I shoved her fist away. "Hey, you know I have asthma. I always have to take this inhaler with me."

"You're totally pumped because you're going to see stars close-up," Cleo Lambeau said. "Look at you. You can't even sit still."

"I *am* sitting still," I said. "It's a bumpy road. The bus keeps bouncing me up and down."

The girls laughed. I sat between them as the school bus rumbled up the narrow mountain road. The three of us had been friends for a long time. You'd think they'd get tired of teasing me. But they don't.

The bus bounced hard. The inhaler flew out of my hand and dropped to the floor. Orly leaned over and picked it up for me.

I pointed out the window. "What's that animal? Did you see it? Was it a mountain lion?"

Cleo sat next to the window. "I think it was a

dog," she said. "Murphy, you're so psyched, you're seeing things!"

"You don't get it," I said. "This isn't a typical school trip. The Rayburne Observatory has one of the most powerful telescopes in the world."

"And you really think you're going to see close-ups of tiny Martians?" Orly said.

"And maybe they'll wave back at you," Cleo added. They both laughed.

"Do you know how funny you're *not*? You've seen too many cartoons," I said. "This is serious."

Serious to *me*, anyway. They could joke all they liked. But my parents took me to see a rocket blast off at NASA in Florida when I was nine, and I've been obsessed with stars and space travel and the universe ever since.

I dream about space travel. And I love writing stories about it.

Here's something I would never tell Orly or Cleo: My big dream is to be an astronaut.

I know. That's kind of sad. I don't think I'd ever be accepted. Mainly because I have asthma and bad allergies, and I have to carry the inhaler at all times.

But I can dream about it, right?

"Listen up, people." Mr. Hawkins, our sixth-grade teacher, stood up and faced us from the front of the bus. He's very tall, so he had to duck his head so he didn't hit the roof.

"We are approaching the observatory." He motioned out the window. "I just want to remind everyone that this is a place of serious science. You've had a long bus ride, and you're probably

8

feeling restless. Like you want to run around and blow off steam."

He shook his head. "But you have to remember that many scientists are doing important work here. So, you need to be serious—and respectful, too—as we enter the observatory."

"Are we getting lunch?" Jesse Halstrom asked. Jesse always likes to know where his next meal is coming from.

"We will have lunch in the observatory cafeteria," Mr. Hawkins said.

"Will it be that freeze-dried astronaut stuff?" Jesse asked.

A lot of kids laughed.

"I think they serve real food," the teacher answered. "As you remember from the videos we watched, the observatory is enormous. Please stick together. Do not wander off on your own. I can't keep track of all of you. And when we return to school, I'd like to bring most of you back with me."

That was a joke. And we all laughed really hard because Mr. Hawkins doesn't make that many jokes.

The bus climbed higher and squealed around a curve. And I could see the huge stone building poking up from the trees above us. My heart started to pound as I gazed at the enormous dome, gleaming under the sunlight.

Orly grabbed my arm. "Your breathing is like an accordion going in and out!" she said. "Calm down."

"We're only going to *see* stars and planets," Cleo said. "We're not going to *visit* them."

She was wrong.

9

We piled off the bus and followed a gray-uniformed guard through the wide glass front doors and into a huge round entryway. Our footsteps echoed off the high stone ceilings.

"This is awesome!" I whispered to Orly and Cleo.

Cleo rolled her eyes. "I thought you might say that."

We heard rapid footsteps ringing out on the marble floor. A man in a long white lab coat came walking out. And I gasped. "It's *him*! It's Sidney Rayburne! I don't believe it. He actually came to greet us himself!"

Cleo raised a finger to her lips. "Murphy, please. You're going to explode if you don't calm down!"

Dr. Rayburne was tall and thin with straight white hair pulled back in a ponytail. He had pale blue eyes behind black square-framed eyeglasses and a white mustache that stuck straight out at the sides. He carried a clipboard in one hand, which he swung as he stepped in front of the class.

I'd read a lot about Sidney Rayburne, but I never expected to be in the same room with him.

10

He designed the amazing telescope that made him famous around the world. And he was in charge of the observatory and all the scientists who worked here.

Some videos I saw said that he was a bit strange and didn't always get along with other astronomers. A lot of people said he was difficult to work with.

He shook hands with Mr. Hawkins, and they said a few words to each other. I was desperate to shake hands with him, too. I knew I would never wash that hand!

He turned to us, and a smile formed beneath the straight mustache. "I am always happy to greet school classes here in my observatory," he said. He had a deep, booming voice that rang off the stone walls. "And I promise you that you will see parts of the universe you have never seen."

"How far can the telescope see in the daytime?" I asked. I couldn't help it. I couldn't hold back my question. My voice came out high and shrill because of my excitement.

"It's the same day or night. My assistants will be explaining everything you want to know," Rayburne replied. "I'm sure that you—"

"How many other galaxies have you seen?" I blurted out.

Rayburne chuckled. "I hope we can answer all your questions later, young man."

"I read that the Salzburg telescope was designed to be more powerful than yours," I said. "Is it true?"

Mr. Hawkins took a few steps toward me. "Murphy, if you could hold your questions till later . . ."

Cleo squeezed my arm hard. "Shhh. What's your problem?"

"Murphy Shannon is a bit of a fanatic," I heard Hawkins tell Dr. Rayburne. "This is the biggest day of his life."

Rayburne's smile grew wide. "I know we won't disappoint you, Murphy."

He gave us a quick wave. "Enjoy your trip to the stars, everyone." Then he turned and walked out of the room.

Two women in white lab coats appeared and led the class into a large, round auditorium. Tiny lights twinkled like stars, high overhead in the domed ceiling. Comfortable movie-theater seats wrapped around the wide circle.

"I am Dr. Gonzalez, and this is Dr. Jackson," one of the women announced. "Sit anywhere you like." She motioned around the circle with one hand. "Our chief astronomer, Dr. Freed, will be here to give you an introduction to the observatory."

I led Cleo and Orly to the back row because it had the best view of the entire ceiling. "This is awesome!" I said. "I'll bet they have amazing light shows up there on the dome."

"Murphy, take a deep breath," Cleo said. "You've really got to chill."

"I hope this astronomer will let us ask questions," I said. "I have a million things I want to know about this place."

"If you have any problem," Dr. Gonzalez said, "or if you need to leave the auditorium for any reason, please see Dr. Jackson or me. Because of security, you will need a guide wherever you go."

Around the room, everyone began talking at once. I wasn't the only kid who was excited. But, of course, I was the *most* excited.

The room grew quiet as Dr. Freed, a tall young man in a dark suit, came stepping into the middle of the circle. He had wavy black hair down to his shoulders, and a short black beard covered most of his face. He wore a red bandanna around his neck in place of a tie, and I saw a silver ring gleam in one ear.

Freed had a tiny microphone clipped to the lapel of his suit jacket, which he tested by poking a finger against it. "Testing . . . testing . . . one . . . two . . . three . . ."

Dr. Gonzalez carried a tall wooden stool to the center of the circle. Dr. Freed lowered himself to the edge of the seat and cleared his throat. "Welcome, everyone," he said. "I am Samuel Freed, and I'm the head astronomer here at the Rayburne Observatory."

He fiddled with the microphone for a few seconds. "We have clear weather on the mountaintop today," he continued. "So I know you kids are going to have some amazing views later."

"Oh, wow," I murmured. I was forcing myself to stay calm. But that was definitely good news.

"I'd like to start out by giving you all a brief history of the telescope," Freed said. As he said that, the twinkling stars disappeared from the domed

13

ceiling. A photo of an old-fashioned telescope took their place. All the other lights in the auditorium went dark.

"In 1609," Dr. Freed continued, "an Italian astronomer named Galileo became the first person to use a telescope aimed at the stars. Even though his telescope was small and primitive, Galileo was able to make out mountains and craters on the moon. In later years . . ."

Freed rattled on about Galileo and Sir Isaac Newton and how telescopes became bigger and sharper. He had a droning voice, and he was reciting everything as if he had said it all a hundred times before.

I poked Cleo in the side. "Come on," I whispered. "I already know all this stuff. Let's get out of here."

Her mouth dropped open. "Sneak out? No way. You heard what they said—"

I motioned to the door right behind us. "Let's just take a short walk. You know. Explore. While he's doing ancient history."

"I'm with you," Orly said. "This is boring."

Cleo crossed her arms in front of her. "I'm not going. They said not to leave."

I grabbed both of them by the arm and tugged them to their feet. I was too excited to sit still. I pulled them to the door, and we slipped out.

"A short walk," I whispered. "Very short. No one will notice we're gone."

Was I making a mistake?

3

"Let go of my arm. I don't want to do this," Cleo said.

Orly was always ready to have fun. But Cleo was the wimp in the group. She was a genius at finding things to be afraid of, like always finding bugs in her food that turned out to be raisins or chocolate chips.

She never went bike riding with Orly and me because "what if I got a flat tire?" When she was home by herself, she turned on every light in the house. I'm not sure why.

Last summer when my parents took the three of us to the beach, Orly and I went racing into the waves. It was so cold, we started to scream.

Cleo stood at the edge of the water, pointing: "Look out! I think I see jellyfish!"

The three of us have been friends for so long, Orly and I don't give Cleo a hard time about being afraid and timid. And I don't know. Maybe it's good to have one friend who is sometimes the sensible one.

I let go of Cleo's arm. "We'll just take a short

walk outside the auditorium," I said. "A minute or two. That's all. Just to stretch our legs."

"You need to stretch your brain," Cleo said. "We don't belong out here."

I pointed up and down the hall. "There's no one here. They must all be in the different labs doing their jobs."

The endless hallway had a dark marble floor and solid stone walls. Wide wooden doors lined the outer wall. They were all closed. The air was cold and smelled sharply of detergent.

I could hear Dr. Freed's droning voice from the loudspeakers in the auditorium. I led the way to the left. "Come on. This is an adventure."

"I don't like adventure," Cleo grumbled. "You know what adventure means? It means trouble."

"It's so quiet out in this hall, you can hear the air," Orly said. She stared up ahead. "There's an open door. Let's see what's there."

Cleo held back, but Orly and I trotted to the open doorway. It opened into a brightly lit room with several glass display cases.

I gazed from wall to wall. They were covered with huge maps. "They're all maps of the universe, I think."

I made my way to the nearest display case. Spread out under the glass was an ancient yellowed scroll. It had the faded outline of an island or maybe a continent on it.

"It must be really old," Orly said, gazing down at it. "Like maybe one of the first-ever maps."

"They should put labels on these maps to identify them," I said.

"They're not really on display, Murphy," Cleo said. "This is a private room, remember? We're not supposed to be in here."

I ignored her and moved to the next case. "This looks like a map of North America," I said. "But the writing all over it is in a foreign language."

"Awesome," Orly murmured.

"Can we go back?" Cleo asked, tugging my arm.

"One more room," I said. "I promise. Just one more room."

We went back into the hall and followed it, passing several more closed doors. I could hear voices behind some of the doors and the hum of large machines.

Another open door revealed a tall glass case in the middle of a brightly lit room. I blinked and gazed at the planets that appeared to be floating inside the case.

"Wow," I muttered. "Check it out. Do you recognize it? It's our galaxy."

Orly stepped up to the glass. "It's in 3-D," she said.

"It's a hologram of the galaxy," I said. "Amazing."

Cleo gasped. "Oh no!"

And then I heard it, too. Footsteps. The click of footsteps approaching the room.

No time to duck or hide. All three of us spun to the door as a woman hurried in. I recognized her from the auditorium. Dr. Jackson.

Her expression grew grim as she eyed us in front of the glass case.

"I—I—I—" I stammered. I couldn't think of an excuse for why we were there.

She raised a finger to her lips. "Listen to me," she said in a choked whisper. She glanced behind her, as if she expected someone to be there.

Suddenly, I realized she looked frightened.

"I'm sorry," I said. "I know we shouldn't—"

"Listen to me," she repeated. "I can only say it once." She glanced behind her again. "Get out of here."

"Okay," I said. "We'll go back. We'll—"

"No!" she cried. "Get out of here. Go home. Get the others and go home . . . while you still have the chance."

My mouth dropped open. Cleo uttered a low cry.

I heard voices out in the hall.

"Dr. Jackson—" I started. But she spun around, her eyes wide with fear, and ran from the room.

The three of us stood frozen in front of the tall glass case. "W-why did she say that?" I stammered.

"She was just trying to scare us," Orly replied.

Cleo raised her hands to her cheeks. "But why? Why did she want to scare us? And why did she say that and then just run away?"

"She knew we didn't belong in here," I said. "And so—"

"So she decided to frighten us to death?" Cleo demanded.

I could see that Orly was thinking hard. "Cleo is right. It's totally strange. Why didn't she take us back to the auditorium?"

I shrugged. "Who knows?" I started to the door. "We'd better get back. Maybe she won't squeal on us."

We stepped into the hallway. In the distance, I saw two women in white lab coats disappear around the curve. I froze and waited to make sure they weren't returning.

"Which way do we go?" Cleo asked. "I got turned around." She shook her head. "I *knew* we'd get lost."

"We're not lost," Orly told her. "We just don't know where we are."

That didn't cheer Cleo up.

Orly motioned to the right. "Isn't that the way we came?"

I gazed in both directions. "No," I said. "I think we came from the other direction."

I led the way. The girls kept shaking their heads. "This doesn't feel right," Cleo whispered.

We passed a few closed doors. A stenciled sign next to a wide glass door read LIBRARY.

"We definitely didn't pass a library," Cleo said. Her voice trembled.

Orly squeezed her hand. "You're shaking. We'll be okay, Cleo. Even if we're lost, we can still—"

"We're not lost," I snapped. "Follow me." We started back toward the galaxy hologram room. "The auditorium should be on our left," I whispered. "We just have to find an entrance."

Cleo shook her head. "I can't believe we did this." Her voice sounded hollow in the long hallway. "All because Murphy wanted an adventure."

"Go ahead. Blame me," I said. "It's not like I forced you two to come."

"Yes, you did," Cleo said.

"Please, don't argue," Orly said. "Let's get back and pretend this didn't happen. We—"

She stopped. We all heard the thud of footsteps. Nearby.

"Over here," I whispered. We burst through an open doorway. The room had bright overhead lights. I saw a tower of computer monitors against the far wall. Laptops, scanners, all kinds of computer equipment.

We darted farther into the room and pressed ourselves against the near wall. My heart was pounding so hard, my breath came out in quick wheezes. I kept my back tight against the wall, the two girls beside me.

We listened as the footsteps passed. "We settled on Florida because it's nearby," a man said.

"And the weather is so nice there," said a woman walking with him.

When their voices faded, I let out a long sigh of relief. "That was close," I said.

"Very close!" a deep voice said from across the room.

I gasped and raised my eyes. We weren't alone.

A gray-haired man in a tan suit stepped out from behind a tall file cabinet.

"Ohhh." Orly let out a startled groan. Cleo stayed pressed against the wall, her eyes wide with fright.

"What are you kids doing in here?" the man demanded. "This room is forbidden to all visitors."

"We—uh—we—" I struggled to speak.

He picked up some kind of radio transmitter and raised it to his face. "Security! Security!" he shouted into it. "Intruders in 1214. Security!"

We bolted to the door and took off running.

If we could only make it back to the auditorium, I knew we could blend in with the other kids and be safe. But I didn't have a clue how to get back there.

We rounded a curve and kept running past closed doors. I knew the auditorium was somewhere on the left side of the hall. But there were no entrance doors.

I uttered a cry when I heard shouts and hard running footsteps behind us. Boots pounding the marble floor.

"Stop right there!" an angry voice boomed.

I turned and glanced back. Three guards were thundering after us. They meant business, I saw. These guys had Tasers!

Cleo was uttering low cries as she ran. Orly was gasping for breath.

"Freeze, you kids! Freeze! We don't want to hurt you!"

We turned a corner, and I stopped at a wide black door. A sign on the door in bold red letters warned: DANGER! PROHIBITED TO ALL!

With a gasp, I lowered my shoulder—and shoved open the door. The three of us scrambled inside and quickly shut the door behind us.

Then I lowered my hands to my knees and struggled to catch my breath.

Cleo and Orly had their eyes closed, mouths open, breathing hard. Their faces were red and drenched in sweat. Their hair stood wild around their faces.

I've never run so hard in my life, I thought, trying to force away the pain in my side. I grabbed my inhaler and gave myself a few fast sprays. Finally, I raised myself back up and gazed around.

The room was filled with awesome electronic equipment. Flashing monitor screens . . . tubes and cables, dark metal machines that hummed and rumbled and clicked.

"Now what?" Cleo cried. "Now what? Now what?"

Orly put a hand on Cleo's shoulder to try to calm her down. But Cleo spun away from her. "Now what? Tell us, Murphy. What's your next bright idea?"

I didn't have a chance to answer.

The door swung open and Dr. Rayburne burst in. He was followed by the three security guards. And they were followed by Dr. Jackson.

Rayburne squinted at us, studying us one at a time. He took several steps into the room. The security guards stood blocking the door. Dr. Jackson stayed a few feet behind Dr. Rayburne.

"Trespassers in the Transition Room," Rayburne said finally. He tsk-tsked. "That's very serious."

"We—we're sorry," I stammered. "We didn't mean to—"

"I found them wandering earlier," Dr. Jackson said. "I told them to get back to the auditorium."

"We'll go back now," Cleo said. "Sorry about the trouble."

"Yes. We apologize for any trouble we caused," Orly added.

I stared hard at Dr. Jackson. "You didn't tell us to go back to our class," I said. "You told us to get away from here as fast as we could."

Dr. Jackson blinked. "No, I didn't. I didn't say that."

"You said we should go home while we still had the chance," I insisted.

She shook her head. "You must have misunderstood me. Why would I say that?"

Dr. Rayburne was studying her now.

"I told you to go back to the auditorium," Dr. Jackson said. "I never said anything about getting away."

Why was she lying?

She and Rayburne stared hard at each other. I could see that Dr. Jackson was afraid of him.

"I'm really sorry, Dr. Rayburne," I said. "We went exploring and got lost. It's just that I'm so totally excited by planets and stars and space travel. I couldn't sit still. And I wanted to explore everything."

"Can we go back to our class now?" Cleo asked.

"I'm sorry. You can't," Rayburne answered. "Your class left. The bus pulled out a few minutes ago."

I gasped. A chill tightened the back of my neck. "N-no!" I stammered.

"That can't be true," Cleo said. "Our class is supposed to stay all day."

Rayburne shook his head. "I know. But sadly, one of the kids got sick, and your teacher had to get everyone on the bus as fast as he could."

"But—but—" I sputtered. "Didn't he see that the three of us—?"

"They left in such a hurry," Rayburne said. "It was an emergency."

Dr. Jackson backed up to the door. She clenched her hands tightly in front of her. Her eyes were wide and kept darting from side to side.

She was definitely frightened.

Behind her, the three security guards stared straight ahead and didn't move.

"We have to get back to school," Orly said. "Can you call the school bus? Call Mr. Hawkins and tell him to turn around?"

Rayburne rubbed a finger over his mustache.

"I'm afraid I don't have a phone number for your teacher," he said softly.

"Are there any taxis that could take us back to school?" I asked.

He snickered. "Taxis? At the top of the mountain? I don't think so."

"Well . . . tell us," Cleo said. "Tell us what to do. We have to get back."

Rayburne's blue eyes flashed behind his eyeglasses. "I have a different destination for you."

"Huh? What do you mean?" I cried.

"You can't go home," he said. "You've seen my Transition Room. You've seen too much."

I could feel panic choking my throat. "But we can't tell anyone about it," I said. "We don't know what any of this equipment does."

"You—you have to send us home!" Cleo's voice cracked with her cry. "Why are you trying to scare us?"

Orly turned to Dr. Jackson. "Will you help us?"

Jackson didn't reply. She backed into the hallway, shaking her head, and vanished from sight.

"This room must remain a secret," Rayburne said. "No one can know about it until I am ready to reveal it to the world—and take my place as one of the greatest scientists in history."

"But—but—you are *already* one of the greatest scientists!" I cried.

A thin smile crossed his face. He tugged at the ends of his white mustache. "I've only just begun," he said. "And now I have you here to make me even more famous."

"But . . . our parents—" I started.

"You can't keep us here!" Cleo shouted.

Orly had her fists balled tightly at her sides. She looked ready for a fight. But I knew that even brave Orly wouldn't try to fight Dr. Rayburne.

Rayburne ignored our protests. "It's lucky that you are interested in outer space," he said. "I am going to honor the three of you and make you famous, too. I'm going to send you *haunting with the stars!*" He chuckled as if he'd just made a great joke.

"Huh? Haunting? Honor us? Wh-what do you mean?" I stammered.

"I'm going to honor you by allowing you to be the very first to travel to a distant planet."

I realized I was wheezing for breath. I pulled out my inhaler and gave myself a few sprays. It helped me feel a little more normal.

Dr. Rayburne was one of the top astronomers in the country. Everyone agreed that his telescope was far more advanced than all the others.

He was a brilliant scientist. So he couldn't be an evil villain.

I suddenly realized what was going on.

"I know what you're doing," I said. "You're deliberately scaring us because you want to punish us. You want to teach us a lesson because we sneaked out of the auditorium and didn't follow instructions."

He pushed the square eyeglasses up on his nose. His eyes narrowed at me. "I'm not trying to scare you," he said. "Didn't you listen to me? I'm going to honor you. This is a prize that people would pay millions to win."

"A—a prize?" I replied.

He nodded. "Think of it, young man. The three of you will be space pioneers. You will be in the history books for all time."

Orly turned to me, her eyes wide, her chin trembling. "He's serious, Murphy," she whispered. "He isn't joking."

Cleo stared hard at Rayburne. "You're going to put us in a rocket ship and send us to another planet?"

For some reason, that made Rayburne chuckle. "A rocket ship?" he said. "How quaint. Rocket ships are too slow for deep space travel."

My mouth dropped open. "Then . . . what—?"

"I knew there had to be a way for people to travel to space without primitive rockets," Rayburne said. He walked up to a tall, gray metal machine covered in dials and twisting cables. He patted it with one hand. "This is it. This is my answer."

The three of us didn't speak. We waited for him to explain.

I kept glancing back at the door. Was there any chance we could escape this room? No. Not with the three guards standing at attention, blocking the whole doorway.

"I can transport people to other planets *instantly*," Rayburne said. He snapped his fingers. "Instantly."

He's crazy, I thought. *We are trapped here with him, and he's crazy!*

He tapped the side of the machine again. "Let me explain. This transition machine will break down your molecules. Then it will send your molecules to the planet I have chosen."

Really crazy.

"Once your molecules have arrived at the other planet, your bodies will quickly re-form."

29

"I think I saw this on *Star Trek*," I said.

Rayburne slammed his fist angrily against the machine. "Don't make jokes, kid. You are about to see historic greatness. Don't make jokes in my presence."

"But that's impossible," Orly said. "Breaking down our molecules? Sending molecules to outer space? Please. Give us a break. Let us go—"

"I *am* letting you go," Rayburne said. "I'm letting you go to a planet I believe is populated—Zoromisis 12."

"Please—" Orly begged again.

"Let us go. It can't work," Cleo said.

"Can't work?" Rayburne tossed both hands in the air. "Can't work? I sent a hippo to Mars! I've sent monkeys to the moon! It works. You will see. You will be the first human space travelers. You will be famous forever—and so will I!"

He motioned to the three security guards. "Hook them up."

No way to escape. My legs were shaking so hard, I didn't think I could even walk.

The guards quickly handcuffed us. A few seconds later, we stood with our backs pressed against a huge machine. I stood between the two girls. All three of us were silent, too frightened to protest or plead or argue with Rayburne.

His mustache twitched as he watched. His mouth was set in a tight grin. His eyes flashed behind the square glasses. I could see he was excited.

Beside me, Cleo had tears in her eyes. Orly chewed her bottom lip and stared straight ahead.

The guards clamped large black headphones over our ears. We didn't try to fight them. We knew there was no point in trying.

A single tear rolled down Cleo's cheek. "I don't want my molecules sent into outer space," she whispered to me.

"Don't worry," I whispered back. "It won't work."

She squinted at me. "What?"

"It won't work," I repeated. "He can't break up our molecules. The whole thing is ridiculous."

"So . . . what's going to happen?" Orly said.

"It's going to fail," I said. "You'll see. When Rayburne discovers that his machine didn't do anything to us, he'll have to let us go."

"I . . . I hope you're right," Cleo whispered.

"Also," I said, "Mr. Hawkins has *got* to realize that we're not on the bus. He'll turn around and come back and rescue us."

Did I believe what I was saying? Or was I just trying to cheer up the three of us and give us some hope?

This is a joke, I thought. *Dr. Rayburne is a brilliant astronomer, one of the top scientists in our country. How can he possibly think that he can use this machine to send people to other planets?*

Why didn't any of the other scientists tell him this was a crazy idea? Why didn't they try to stop him from working on this?

"Travel time," Rayburne said. He ordered the guards to strap our feet to the machine. Then he moved to a desk and sat down behind a large desktop computer. He tapped for a while on the keyboard, and then he raised his head, peering at us over the monitor.

"Ready?" he said. "You may feel a slight tingling. But there won't be any pain. At least I don't think so."

He lowered his face behind the monitor and typed some more.

"Don't worry," I whispered to the girls. "Nothing is going to happen to us. Trust me."

They both stared at me and didn't reply.

"These headphones can't do anything to us," I

said. "They're just headphones. We're going to be perfectly okay."

Rayburne typed some more. The machine let out a shrill tweeting sound. Like birds chirping.

"See?" I whispered to the girls. "It isn't going to work."

The tweeting rang in my ears. Rayburne climbed up from his seat. He stepped up to the side of the machine and grabbed a lever in both hands.

"Here we go!" he cried. "Happy travels!"

He pushed the lever down hard.

And the big machine roared to life.

9

The roar grew louder in the headphones, and I could feel the machine vibrating. The sound rose until my ears started to hurt. I held my breath. I could feel the vibrations pulsing through my whole body.

Cleo, Orly, and I huddled close together, the machine rumbling now, shaking and rumbling. Cleo was screaming something, but I couldn't hear her over the machine. I saw her whole body shudder.

Whoa. I reached out to try to calm her—and a shout escaped my throat.

My hand!

Where was my hand?

My arm ended at the wrist. And as I stared in horror, the wrist disappeared . . . the arm disappeared . . . My shirtsleeve . . . the sleeve . . . it was *gone*!

"Nooooooo." Was that me groaning like that?

The machine vibrated and shook. I pressed my back against it harder, struggling to keep my balance. But when I lowered my gaze, I saw that my shoes were gone . . . My feet . . . they had vanished!

My legs started to fade.

Is this happening?

I turned to Cleo. *Where was her head?*

Her shoulders quivered under her sweater. She tried to raise her arms . . . Her hands . . . and then her sweater vanished. And then . . . she vanished.

"Nooo! Noooo! Noooo!"

That had to be *me* screaming. Because the two girls were no longer at my sides.

I saw my legs float off my body . . . float in front of me . . . I had no hands to grab them with.

I stared in disbelief as my legs dissolved. Like liquid. And then like powder.

I'm coming apart . . . I'm dissolving . . . fading now . . . fading . . .

I wanted to scream more, but I no longer had a voice. Did I still have a head? I wasn't sure. I didn't know. I didn't know anything.

And then I was gone.

SLAPPY HERE, EVERYONE.

Well ... Murphy said he loved everything about space. And now there's a *lot* of space where his clothing used to be! Hahaha.

One thing he should have remembered when he went exploring: He should have remembered to keep his head!

Take it from your old pal Slappy, friends. Togetherness is important.

Especially togetherness with your arms and legs! Hahaha!

Hope Murphy, Cleo, and Orly can get it together.

Otherwise, this could be a very short book! Haha!

A white mist swirled around me. I heard the rush of a soft wind.

Were my eyes open or closed? I tried to blink, but I couldn't see through the billowing fog.

"Am I alive?"

I heard my voice. It sounded far away, as if I was talking from somewhere outside me. The rush of the wind grew louder.

"Where am I? Am I alive?"

My throat ached. So dry. I struggled to swallow.

I raised both hands and tried to rub the fog from my eyes. I could hear muffled sounds in the distance, like the honking of geese. And then a chirping sound—*chit-chit-chit*—I didn't recognize.

If only I could see!

I swallowed again and spoke to myself. "Murphy, you are alive. Murphy, you are here. But—where?"

I spun around. The thick mist surrounded me. I couldn't see through the heavy curtain of fog.

"Where am I? Is anyone there? Can anyone see me?"

The strange chirping sounds repeated. The wind seemed to ease up. And the fog slowly lifted.

I rubbed my eyes again and squinted into a bright pink light. I seemed to be looking down on low, round caves. No, wait. Windows came into focus. They weren't caves. They were buildings, some kind of huts.

Was I standing on a hill? The pale pink sky rose high around me. The buildings down below were a deep purple. *Chit-chit-chit.* Were those *birds* chirping all around me?

I took a deep breath. The air smelled sweet. I began to feel more like myself. I gazed up at a dark pink sun high in the sky.

I heard voices from the buildings down below. Deep, croaking frog voices. I couldn't make out the words.

Where am I? How did I get here?

I suddenly realized I wasn't alone. I lowered my eyes to the ground. The hill was covered in clumps of thick gray grass. An animal popped up from one of the clumps and stared at me.

A squirrel? No. It had six legs!

"Hey—" I called to it. It spun away from me and went scrambling down the hill, all six legs running at once.

"Whoa." I suddenly saw flashes of Dr. Rayburne's lab. The Transition Room. Strapped to the roaring machine, headphones over my ears. Molecules dissolving . . .

"No!" A cry burst from my throat.

Did Rayburne's machine work? Did it really send me to a distant planet?

Did my molecules really fly apart, sail through

the atmosphere, and come together somewhere in outer space? Or was this some kind of trick?

My brain spun with questions. Here I was on this grassy hillside under a strange pink sky. Looking down on a village of round purple huts.

The huts stretched away from the hill in straight lines. I squinted hard, struggling to focus. Those had to be streets between the huts.

Strange, low vehicles slid rapidly up and down the streets. They were gray and they were shaped like vitamin capsules. They had no tires or wheels, but they scooted silently ahead.

I saw figures moving along the streets, in and out of the small round buildings. Were they people? I was too far away to see them clearly.

My eyes burned from the pink sunlight. I raised a hand to rub them—and gasped.

My hand—I couldn't see it.

I stared, blinking in shock. My arms . . . my clothes . . . my shoes . . .

"I'm invisible!" I cried out loud. My voice carried down the hillside.

I'm here. I'm definitely standing here.
But I'm invisible.

I squeezed my arm. I pinched my nose. I bounced up and down on my feet.

Yes. I could feel things.

"I'm real!" I shouted. A crazy thing to scream. But I couldn't hold back my shock, my confusion.

I saw a blur of motion where my feet should have been visible. Another six-legged squirrel. It ran right into my ankle, then bounced away.

That animal can't see me, either.

My heart was pounding hard in my chest. I took a deep breath and held it. My brain was whirring. I tried to focus, tried to slow my racing thoughts.

Cleo. Orly. I could picture their faces floating before my eyes.

They had been beside me, hooked up to Rayburne's machine. The three of us stood there trembling as he told us his wild plans.

I told the girls his idea would never work. But here I was, invisible under this pink sun, gazing at six-legged squirrels, cars shaped like pills, and rows of round purple buildings.

He did it. Rayburne wasn't crazy. He really sent me to another planet.

This was amazing! This was unbelievable! This was . . . *thrilling*!

But where were the girls?

"Orly!" I cried. "Cleo!" My voice sounded hoarse. I could hear their names ringing down the hill. "Are you here? Where are you?"

A burst of wind was my only reply.

"Orly! Can you hear me? Cleo?" I shouted. "I'm here. I'm invisible, but I'm here!" I spun all the way around. "Where are you? Answer me! Please!"

Silence.

I waited, holding my breath. Waited to hear their voices.

But no. No answer to my shouts.

I told myself to be brave, but my whole body shuddered and a sob escaped my throat.

I was alone now. Maybe on a distant planet millions of miles from Earth.

Were the girls hurt? Were their molecules scattered through space? Would I ever see them again?

"All my fault," I muttered. "If I hadn't pulled them out into the hall . . ."

Alone. All alone.

And . . . *now what*?

11

As the dark pink sun lowered in the sky, three half-moons appeared around it. The air grew cooler. I wished I had my hoodie, but it was back at Rayburne's observatory. I couldn't see my clothes. But I remembered I was wearing a T-shirt and jeans.

I gazed down the hill. The gray grass shifted from side to side, blown by the wind. I realized I had no choice. I had to walk down to that village of round huts and find out where I was.

I'd taken three or four steps, slipping on the wet grass, when I heard a girl's voice. "Is anyone there?"

It was Orly! I spun around, but I didn't see her.

"Is anyone there? Murphy? Cleo?"

She stood close behind me.

"Orly! You're here!"

"Murphy! Where are you?" she called. "I can't see you!"

"I can't see either of you!" Cleo said. Her voice floated down from higher on the hill.

"You're here! You're both here!" I cried. "Whoa. I'm so happy. I thought—"

"Where is *here*?" Cleo said. "Where are we?"

"I don't know," I answered. "Maybe we're on that planet Rayburne said he'd send us to. Or maybe we're in Ohio or something. How can we know for sure?"

"It doesn't look like Ohio," Orly said. "I mean . . . the pink sun and three moons . . ." Her voice faded.

"Why are we invisible?" Cleo demanded. "Are we going to stay this way forever?"

That thought sent a chill to the back of my neck. "We can stand here asking a lot of questions," I said. "But we can't answer any of them. We don't know where we are. And we don't know why we can't see each other."

"I guess that's some kind of village down there," Orly said. "We have no choice. We have to go down there and see if we can find some answers."

"Orly is right. We have to go down there," Cleo said in a whisper. And then she added, "Are you two as scared as I am?"

"Yes!" Orly and I both answered at once.

"Let's go," I said. "Follow me."

"How can we follow you?" Cleo asked. "We can't see you."

I reached my hand out and moved it around till I felt her hand. "Orly, find us," I said. "We'll hold hands and keep talking all the way down. That way, we'll know we're walking together."

Orly's hand thumped my shoulder. I reached up and grabbed it.

"I have just one more question," Cleo said. "How do we get back? How do we get back home?"

A long silence as the three of us thought about it.

Then, in a trembling voice, I said, "Rayburne never said anything about bringing us back."

12

Holding hands, we started to walk down the hill. I kept stumbling over the clumps of strange grass because I couldn't see my feet. Once, Cleo's hand slipped out of mine, and it took a long time to find it again.

We kept talking all the way down, chattering nervously, trying to keep it together. "Rayburne said we would be famous," Orly said. "If we really are on a distant planet . . . he *has* to bring us back to show the world what he has done."

"I . . . I hope you're right," I stammered. My chest suddenly felt tight. I could breathe the air here, but I began to feel out of breath. I raised my inhaler and sent a few puffs into my lungs.

"We should try to get as much information as we can," I said. "You know. Learn about life here. While we wait for Rayburne to bring us back."

"But . . . what if he doesn't know how?" Cleo demanded. Always the biggest worrier. "What if he only knows how to *send* people places? What about our parents? What about our friends?" Her voice grew more and more shrill. "Will we ever see them again?"

Cleo being Cleo.

"Let's try not to think about all that," Orly said.

"What *should* we think about?" Cleo snapped.

"Lunch," Orly said. "We didn't have any lunch at the observatory, remember?"

"Maybe there are restaurants in this town," I said. The round purple buildings were closer now. They were a lot taller than they appeared up on the hill. The capsule-shaped cars slid silently up and down the streets.

"Do you have any money?" Cleo asked. "I didn't bring any. How can we buy lunch?"

That made me laugh. "Cleo, if we actually are on a distant planet, what makes you think they use our dollars?"

It took her a while to reply. "You're right, Murphy," she said finally. "So we can't buy lunch. We're going to starve."

"Maybe there are nice people in this town, and they'll feed us," Orly said.

I laughed again. "People? Do you really think there are people like us here? They might be creatures . . . creatures who don't look anything like Earth people."

"Shut up, Murphy," Cleo said. "Just stop saying things like that. You're only scaring me worse."

At the bottom of the hill, the wide road began, leading through rows of the purple buildings. We stopped at the edge of the road and listened.

"What's that tapping sound?" Orly asked.

"Maybe a woodpecker?" Cleo said. "We have a woodpecker behind our house that taps like that."

The steady tapping rang in my ears. It seemed to bounce off the sides of the buildings.

"Sounds like dozens of woodpeckers," I said.

We stepped onto the road and followed it to the first building. It appeared to be some kind of shop. I walked up to the display window in front and stared at piles of yellow ropy things, all knotted together.

What were those things?

I didn't have time to think about it. I jumped back as the front door slid open and two figures came out. They moved quickly, their feet tapping the road, coming right at us.

"Oh, wow!" Cleo cried. "There *are* people here!"

"P-people?" I stammered. "Are you sure they're people? Take another look at them!"

"They have two heads!" Cleo screamed.

"Shhh. Not so loud," I said. "They'll hear you."

But the two creatures didn't turn around. The four heads all seemed to be talking at once.

I pressed myself against the front of the building and studied them. They stood like humans and had two arms and two legs like humans. But they each had two heads rising up on two slender necks from their shoulders.

They both wore white outfits, pants and tops, very loose-fitting like pajamas. All four heads were bald. The taller one had what appeared to be yellow flowers growing out of the top of his head.

As I watched them move past us, I realized what caused the tap-tap-tapping sound all around us. Their feet looked like animal hooves, like goat hooves. And they weren't walking. They were dancing. *Tap-tap-tap*. Like tap dancing. The hooves clicked loudly on the pavement.

"More of them," Cleo said. "Look. Across the street."

A capsule car rolled past. I turned to see three more of the creatures dancing along the other side of the street. One was bald and two of them had yellow flowers poking up from their scalps.

The bald one's two heads were shouting at each other. They looked like they were having an argument.

"I can't hear what they're saying," Cleo said. "The tap dancing drowns out their voices. Can you hear them?"

"They probably don't speak English," I said. "How could we understand them even if we could hear?"

"Do you think the ones with flowers on their heads are girls?" Orly asked.

The question made me laugh. Here we were on a distant planet, watching creatures no one on Earth had ever seen, and I just realized—why would we think there'd be boys and girls here?

"They all dress alike in those white pajamas," Cleo said. "Maybe everyone is the same on this planet."

The shop door swung open again, and a creature tapped out onto the street. This one was much shorter than the others we had seen. Maybe a kid? Both heads were wearing flat white caps.

"You are looking great today," one head said to the other.

"No. *You* are looking great," the other head said.

"No. You are looking much greater than me. I look tired today," the first head replied.

"You don't look tired," the other head said. "I look tired. You look greater than me."

They danced along the street, arguing about which of them looked better.

I realized I was gasping for breath. "Did you

hear that?" I asked the girls. "We—we can *understand* them!"

"Amazing!" Orly exclaimed. "They speak English! That's totally good news."

I thought about it for a moment. "I don't think they speak English," I said. "I think Rayburne did something to our thought molecules. I think he probably messed with our brains so we can understand alien languages."

"So, they won't be able to understand what we say?" Cleo said.

"Who knows?" I answered.

"Well, we have to try to talk to them," Orly said. "We can't just stand here and watch them."

Another short creature passed by, hooves tapping loudly on the pavement. Its two heads were talking about what a warm day it was. "It's a three-moon night," said one head. "That means it will soon cool down."

"Yes. We have to talk to them. Maybe they can help us," Cleo said. "Maybe they can tell us where we are and how we can get back home."

"And how to get some food," Orly added. "I'm seriously starving."

"But . . . we're still invisible," I said. "They can't see us. They dance right past us and don't know we're here."

"But they can probably *hear* us," Cleo argued.

"Okay," I said. "Let's stop one of them and talk to it."

I swallowed, suddenly nervous. Was I really about

to become the first person in history to talk with an alien on a distant planet?

The short alien had stopped in front of another shopwindow. The two heads were talking about something they saw in the window. Their feet kept tapping as they stood in place.

I stepped up beside them and cleared my throat loudly. "Hello," I said. "Can you hear me? My friends and I just arrived here. Can you help us?"

14

"That would look better on you than on me," one head said to the other.

"I can't wear that," the other head replied. "It's not my color."

They both had scratchy, hoarse voices.

"Can you hear me?" I tried again. "I know you can't see me. But my friends and I would really like to talk to you."

"You could ask inside," one head said to the other. "Maybe they have it in a different color."

"I really don't want to," came the reply. "I already have two of them anyway."

I turned to where I thought the girls were standing. "They can't hear me," I said. "They can't see me and they can't hear me."

"Let me try," Orly said. And she screamed at the top of her lungs. "Hello! Hello! Can you hear us? Please answer!"

The two heads took one last look in the shopwindow. Then the creature turned and tap-danced away, hooves clicking loudly on the hard street.

"There *has* to be a way to communicate with

them," Cleo said, her voice cracking. "There *has* to."

"Let's think about it," I said.

"I'm too hungry to think," Orly moaned. "There *has* to be something to eat on this street."

"I've dreamed about space travel my whole life," I said. "And now here we are, and it isn't anything like I thought it would be." I sighed. "Wish I had my phone. I should be taking a thousand photos!"

We started walking. We passed a shop with white pajamas in the window. Then a shop with tall bottles in the window. The bottles all had *two* straws in them.

"That store sells drinks," Cleo said. "Maybe they have food, too."

We started toward the door, but something across the street caught my eye. Two of the aliens tapped out of a building, holding some kind of food on sticks. The heads crunched away as they danced down the street.

"That's definitely a food place," I said. "Maybe it's some kind of restaurant or something. Let's check it out."

"Whoa. Hold on. Wait," Cleo said. I felt her tug my arm.

"What's wrong?" I said.

"Everything," she said. "What if it *is* a restaurant or a food store? How are we going to pay?"

I thought hard. "Maybe everything is free."

"But what if it isn't free?" Cleo said. "What do we do?" Always the worrier.

"I don't care," Orly groaned. "My stomach is growling like it's angry at me. We've got to get food."

"But—" I started.

"Look. We're invisible, right?" Orly said. "We're invisible and they can't hear us. We're like ghosts. We can take any food we want, and they won't be able to see us or hear us or catch us."

"Okay," I said. "Let's give it a try. What have we got to lose?"

Was that a stupid question?

We soon found out.

We stepped through the open shop door. The air inside felt warm and smelled like . . . I don't know *what* it smelled like. I'd never smelled that aroma before. Kind of sweet and peppery and minty at the same time.

A two-headed creature in white pajamas stood behind a long glass food counter. He was dropping a pile of bright pink food into a customer's open hands.

I guess they don't have bags here, I thought.

An open food bar stood in the middle of the shop. I walked over to it and gazed at piles of pink and yellow items in one section. Were they vegetables? Fruits? Some were straight like carrots. Other foods were curled up like worms.

"I don't suppose we can get sandwiches here," Orly grumbled.

"Shhh," I whispered. I turned to the guy behind the counter. We had to make sure he couldn't hear us. We didn't want to be caught stealing in our first hour in town.

"Hello!" I shouted. "Hello! Can you hear me?"

He waved good-bye to the customer, who turned

and tap-danced away, holding the pile of food between his hands.

"We are new here!" I shouted. "And we're very hungry. Can we help ourselves to food?"

The two heads muttered to each other. One had short blond fuzz on top. The other was bald. They chuckled about something. At least I think it was chuckling. It sounded more like coughing than laughing.

The store clerk took out a rag and began mopping the top of the counter. The two heads kept chattering to each other.

"They can't hear us," Orly said. "And they can't see us. Let's try to eat something from this case."

"I . . . I don't see anything I like," Cleo stammered. "It all looks like worms and sticks. Is it raw? Is it cooked?"

I poked a yellow pile of something—and it *moved*! "It's ALIVE!" I cried.

Orly made a gagging sound. "Their food is alive? Do we have to kill it before we eat it?"

"I . . . I can't," Cleo said. "I'm feeling sick. I'm going back outside."

"You have to be brave," I said. "We don't know how long we're going to be here. We don't want to starve."

"I'd rather starve than swallow something that's alive," Cleo said. "Uggggh. I can just imagine it wiggling on my tongue."

Another customer tap-danced into the store, hooves clicking rapidly on the hard floor. Both heads had yellow flowers poking up from the scalps. The new customer's hooves kept tapping as he studied the long food display.

"I'm going to try this blue thing that looks like an apple," Orly said. I saw the blue thing float up from the case. I heard Orly bite down on it.

"Ewww!" she cried. "It's sooo slimy! Ohhh." She made loud spitting sounds, and a blue chunk flew out and hit the floor.

"L-let's go," Cleo stammered. "I mean, really. I'm going to barf."

I turned toward the door—then stopped. Behind the front counter, the store clerk was pointing at us.

"Oh no! He saw the blue food float! We're caught!" I cried.

16

I heard Orly and Cleo gasp.

I froze.

The store clerk said something to the customer and kept pointing toward us. Then I saw him pick up a long knife.

"Oh no . . ." I moaned.

The store clerk stepped around the counter and came walking toward us with the knife raised in front of him.

"L-let's go!" Cleo stammered. She grabbed my arm and started to pull me to the door.

I wanted to move. But my legs wouldn't work. I was frozen in fright.

The clerk stepped up to the food bar and lowered the knife to a container of long blue wormlike things. He sliced off a section and handed it to the customer.

The customer nodded both heads and began to chew the food up noisily.

"He . . . he doesn't see us," I told the girls. "He didn't see the blue food floating. He was pointing to the food table—not to us."

The customer began shoving more blue worms into his two mouths.

"Let's get out of here," I said. "That was a close one. There's got to be somewhere else we can get food."

"Maybe this town has pizza," Orly said. "Every place has pizza—right?"

Cleo laughed. "Dream on."

We started through the door and nearly bumped into two more customers tap-dancing in. The shop seemed to be a popular place.

The street had become more crowded. The capsule cars slid by in a line. The drumbeat of the tapping hooves was nearly deafening. I covered my ears and gazed around.

The next shop also had white pajamas in the front window. The shop beside it appeared to be a hat shop. White caps were displayed in sets of two. They rested on wooden mannequin heads, like department store dummies.

I studied them for a moment. The caps had holes on the top so that flowers could poke through.

A couple came hurrying toward us, all four heads talking at once. We had to leap out of the way so they wouldn't bump right into us.

"Hey—watch where you're going!" I shouted.

But, of course, they didn't hear me.

Two of the heads were chewing at long black tubes that looked like licorice. "Those look good," Orly said. "I wonder where they got them."

"Maybe across the street," Cleo said. She pointed to a shop with a wide glass window. The pink sun reflected in the glass so that I couldn't see what was inside.

We waited for some capsule cars to slide past. Then we crossed the street, careful not to collide with the tap-dancing creatures. I peered into the wide front window.

The place was crowded with people seated at long planks, like picnic tables. They all seemed to have piles of food in front of them, and they shoved the stuff into their mouths as they kept talking.

"It's like a cafeteria," Orly said. "They probably have cooked food here."

"How do we know?" Cleo warned.

"If it isn't moving, I'm going to try it," Orly replied.

"Okay. Let's go in," I said.

The glass doors slid open as we stepped up to them. "The doors can see us, but the people can't," I said. "How weird is that?"

"Everything is weird now," Cleo murmured. "Everything in our lives. If only Dr. Rayburne would bring us home. What is taking him so long?"

I didn't answer. Thinking about Rayburne and how maybe he stuck us here for good . . . It just made me feel more frightened.

We walked inside. I could see that it was a big food hall. The voices were so loud with two-headed conversations, my ears rang. Workers behind a long food counter were dishing out steaming plates of food.

Screechy music roared over the crowd noise. It didn't sound like music. It sounded like screaming, howling cats.

We moved closer to the food counter. "It doesn't smell too bad," Orly said.

"At least it looks cooked!" Cleo said. "Maybe it doesn't taste horrible."

Ahead of us, a big creature was piling food onto two trays, one in each hand. I stepped up beside him and sniffed a food tray. Not bad. It was brown and looked like some kind of meat patty. Maybe like a hamburger?

I started to reach for one on the counter but stopped when Cleo whispered, "I just had a thought. If we eat something, will they be able to see it inside us?"

"Huh?" I turned to her voice. "Cleo, what are you worrying about now? I don't understand."

"We're invisible, right?" she answered. "But the food isn't invisible. So if we swallow some, will they be able to see it in our stomachs?"

"Let's try it and find out. I'll make sure no one is looking this way so they won't see it floating," Orly said. "I'm going to taste one of those little round things. They look like dumplings."

"Hope it's good," I said.

I watched as one of the little round dumplings appeared to float up quickly from its dish. I knew Orly was raising it to her mouth.

I held my breath and watched as it disappeared.

"Well? How is it?" I asked.

No answer.

"Orly? How is it?" I repeated.

No answer.

"Orly?" Cleo and I both screamed her name. "What's wrong?"

"Give me a break," she said finally. "I was chewing. It's very chewy."

"Well, what does it taste like?" I demanded.

"It's not bad," she said. "It's kind of salty. Tastes a little like popcorn."

"Popcorn? Seriously?" Cleo said.

I saw a dumpling float up and disappear into Cleo's mouth.

"I could eat a dozen of these," Orly said. Another dumpling floated off the food counter.

"Well, go ahead, Murphy. Try it," Cleo said. "What are you waiting for?"

I reached out and grabbed a dumpling—but I didn't raise it to my mouth. "Ohhhhh—wait!" I cried.

"What's your problem?" Orly asked.

"I—I—I—" I stammered. I couldn't get the words out.

"Murphy? What's wrong?" Cleo said.

"I—I can *see* you!" I cried.

They turned to each other and both screamed in shock.

"We're back!" Cleo said. "We're visible!"

And while I stared openmouthed at the two girls, my hand popped into view. And then both of my arms appeared. And I gazed down at my T-shirt and jeans. I was back, too.

"Uh-oh." I uttered a gasp when I saw the workers behind the food counter turn. They began blinking their eyes and squinting at us, all heads suddenly talking at once.

I heard a stirring across the food hall. Chairs scraped. Cries of surprise rang over the big room.

I let the dumpling fall from my hand. The food workers began moving toward us.

More chairs scraped as people jumped to their hooves.

"They see us! They all see us!" I said.

Yes, everyone in the enormous food hall was staring at us now. And before we could do anything ... before we could move ... the angry shouts rose up from all around.

"One-headers!"

"One-headers! Invaders!"

"Look at them! One-headers!"

"Get them! Get them!"

"They're coming for us!" I cried. "Let's get out of here!"

Orly grabbed two more dumplings and popped them into her mouth. I grabbed her arm and began to tug her toward the front door. Cleo ran close behind.

But the diners were all out of their seats now and tapping toward us. All their heads were raised in angry cries, loud bleating sounds, like howling goats.

"Stop them!"

"Stop the one-headers!"

No way we could burst through them and get to the door.

I spun back to the long food counter. "This way!" I cried. I spread both hands on the top and did a cartwheel over the counter. Orly and Cleo scrambled after me. We headed for a set of swinging double doors at the back of the room.

The food servers, bleating their heads off, came thundering at us.

I lowered my shoulder and shoved open the doors.

The three of us darted into a brightly lit kitchen. A few cooks in white chef uniforms stood working at tall wall ovens, their backs turned.

"Look for an exit!" I whispered to the girls.

We ducked low behind a kitchen counter and moved toward the back. But we hadn't ducked low enough.

I heard a shout. "One-headers!"

"Oh no! Catch them! Catch the ugly beasts! Quick!"

I heard their tapping hooves on the floor as they came charging at us.

"Run!" I cried.

I stood up straight, spun around the corner of the counter—and ran head-on into a loaded food cart. The cart toppled onto its side and hit the floor with a deafening crash.

Trays of food went flying in all directions, an explosion of pinks and yellows. The clatter and splash drowned out the cries of the cooks.

I stumbled over a pool of slimy yellow noodles. Cleo grabbed my hand to keep me on my feet, and we staggered toward the row of sinks at the back.

Both heads bleating like ambulance sirens, a large cook dove at us. He leaped high and spread his arms as if to tackle all three of us.

We scurried just out of his reach. He hit the floor on his belly and went sliding over the pool of spilled yellow food.

"Stop! One-headers! Stop!"

"Catch those creatures!"

Behind us, the double doors swung open and

workers burst in, shouting and bleating, their eyes darting wildly around the kitchen until they spotted us. Then they turned and came tap-dancing toward us, shaking their fists in the air.

"T-there's no door!" Cleo stammered. "We're trapped. We can't get away."

I glanced around the big kitchen and spotted an open window at the far wall. "Over there! Go!" I pointed to the window and took off.

"It's no use!" Cleo cried. "Murphy, stop! If we get away from them, someone else will catch us outside. We don't stand a chance."

Typical Cleo.

"No!" I shouted. "Just follow me. I have a plan."

I grabbed for the window ledge. But I didn't make it. A huge red-faced cook grabbed me, wrapped his arms around me, and tackled me to the floor.

19

The cook landed heavily on my back and pushed me facedown against the floor.

I struggled and squirmed—and managed to spin onto my back.

I stared up at his angry red faces, his four bulging eyes. He grabbed my shoulders with big hands and pressed them against the floor.

"I'm going to see you in my nightmares," one of his heads said.

"Where did you come from? How can you walk around like that?" the other head said.

I tried to pull myself up. But he was too strong. "Let go! Let me up!" I cried.

Then I saw Orly creep up behind him. *Be careful*, I thought. *You're not strong enough to pull him off me.*

But she didn't try to tug him away. She leaned over and lowered both hands—and began to tickle his necks.

His four eyes bulged in surprise. His mouths dropped open.

Orly tickled away, fierce two-handed tickling.

And the cook began to giggle. His giggle became a laugh. And in a few seconds, both heads were choking with laughter.

His hands loosened on my shoulders—just enough for me to roll away. I jumped to my feet. The cook lay sprawled on his back, laughing.

Nice work, Orly!

I bent my knees and sprang up high. I dove out the window before the other two-headers in the room could get to us. I landed hard on my elbows and knees on the pavement outside. Ignoring the pain, I jumped to my feet.

Orly sailed out after me. I caught her by the arms and kept her from falling.

"Cleo? Cleo? Where are you?" My cry floated out, high and shrill.

I leaned into the window—and saw that two of the creatures were holding Cleo by the arms. She struggled and squirmed, but they held on tight.

My breath caught in my throat. I could feel the panic roll down my body like a heavy wave.

"HEY!" I screamed into the window. "LOOK BEHIND YOU!"

Could they understand me? I don't know.

I guess they *did* understand. Because it worked. The two creatures turned to look behind them, and Cleo broke free of their grasp.

With a loud cry, she leaped headfirst out the window—and crashed into me. "Owwww!" A scream burst from my throat.

We both went down in a heap and frantically

scrambled to get up. Orly pulled Cleo off me just as
a few of the angry creatures burst up to the window.

"Are they coming after us?" Orly cried.

"We have to hide s-somewhere!" Cleo stammered.

I grabbed her hand and pulled. "Follow me."

I led them into the street. A long silver capsule
car squealed to a stop. I could hear the driver shouting at us. Another capsule sped past in the other
direction.

All three of us were breathing hard as we reached
the other side. I glanced back. No one was following us.

"Now what?" Cleo demanded.

"Into this shop," I said. "You'll see."

We shot into the clothing shop. The walls were
black, and the lights were dim. It took a while for
my eyes to adjust from the bright pink sunlight outside. I squinted down the long aisle in the middle of
the store.

"We may be in luck," I whispered. "I don't see
anyone around."

Cleo elbowed me in the side. "What's your bright
idea, Murphy? What are we doing in here?"

"Shhh." I held a finger to my lips. I kept glancing down the aisle, hoping no shop workers would
appear. "We can get disguises here."

The two girls exchanged glances. "Disguises?"

I walked over to a long rack of white pajamas.
"Everyone seems to be wearing these," I whispered.
"We've got to blend in with everyone else. Try to
find a pair that fits. Hurry."

69

I grabbed a pair off the rack and held it up in front of me. "Too short."

I held up the next pair. Then the next. "This is long, but I can roll up the cuffs," I said.

At the other end of the rack, the girls found pajamas that almost fit.

"Quick—pull them on," I whispered.

"What do we do with *our* clothes?" Cleo asked.

"Just toss them in the corner," I said, pointing. I pulled my inhaler from my jeans pocket and tucked it into the pajama pants pocket. Then I started to take off my jeans.

But I stopped when something fell out of my back pocket.

I heard it clatter to the floor. I bent quickly to pick it up. A small black box. About the size of a cell phone.

How did it get in my pocket? I raised it close. And saw a red button on one end. And in tiny type above the red button I read the words: PRESS HERE.

20

No time to study the little box. No time to show it to the girls. We had to get out of that shop before we were caught.

I shoved my clothes in a bundle into the dark corner. In seconds, all three of us stood in our white pajamas, looking like we belonged on this planet.

"But you forgot one thing, Murphy," Cleo said. "We still have only one head."

"I've got that covered, too," I told her.

I led them to the front window. We gazed at the display of white caps. They were in sets of two. Each hat rested on top of a mannequin head. The heads had real-looking eyes and red painted smiles. Each head rested on a wooden stick.

"Here are our extra heads," I said. "It's so lucky that their faces look like ours. I think we can fool them. I think—"

I jumped when I heard a sound behind us. My breath caught in my throat as I saw a salesclerk tap-dance out from behind a curtain at the far wall.

She had a load of white pajamas bundled in her arms. "Can I help you?" she asked.

I knew we were caught. How long would it take her to see we were one-heads? That we were stealing clothes?

"Just looking around!" I called back to her.

She turned to the wall of shelves in back. "If I can help, let me know," one of her heads said.

I realized she hadn't looked at us. Too busy with the pile of pajamas.

Maybe . . . just maybe, my plan would work.

I grabbed a mannequin head, raised it to my shoulders, and stuck the stick down the collar of my pajama shirt. I turned the head till it faced straight forward. Then I grabbed two white caps and placed one on my head and one on the mannequin head.

"Ta-da!" I whispered to the girls. "Check it out. I'm a two-header!"

Cleo shook her head and frowned. "I don't think so."

"Maybe it will work," Orly said. She lifted a mannequin head from the display and pushed the stick down her collar until the head rested next to her real head.

Cleo shook her head. "What about our feet? Our feet will give us away! They don't look like hooves."

"We just have to hope the creatures don't look down at them," I said. "These mannequin heads are the only choice we have."

Cleo sighed. "I guess it's worth a try."

I helped her tug her second head into place. Then I set white caps on both heads.

"Keep your caps low," I said. "That makes it hard to see the mannequin face." I took a deep breath.

"Maybe it will work—at least until Rayburne decides to rescue us."

"Well . . . we'll soon find out," Cleo said.

I took one last glance at the salesclerk, who still had her heads turned.

"We'll come back later," I called to her.

Then the three of us new two-headers stepped back out into the street.

"Hey—!" a deep voice cried. "Wait right there!"

21

A tall two-headed creature tap-danced quickly toward us.

He stopped a few feet away. His two heads studied us. One of his faces was thin and pale and serious-looking. His other face was red and round and smiling.

"Can I ask you something?" the serious head said in a deep voice.

"Did you just come out of that shop?" the other head demanded.

I nodded. I bent my shoulders so that my second head would nod, too. But he was staring hard at all three of us. Was he looking at our fake heads?

"Yes," Orly answered. "We just came out."

"How is it?" the creature asked. "Is it good?"

"Someone told us it was very expensive," his other head said.

I coughed. "No. Not expensive at all."

"Actually, it was very cheap," Orly added. "They were practically *giving* everything away!"

It was hard to keep a straight face. I bent my shoulders again to make my second head nod.

The creature turned to the shopwindow. "I need some new hats," he said. He pointed to the two caps he was wearing. "Mine were left out in a padrizzle and lost their shape."

"They have good caps in there," I said.

What's a padrizzle?

The guy's heads said thank you, and he hurried into the shop.

Cleo, Orly, and I burst out laughing. "We totally fooled him," Orly said. "Murphy, you're a genius!"

More creatures passed us on the street. No one looked at us twice. A capsule car pulled to a stop. The top slid open and two creatures climbed out. They tap-danced past us without even looking at us.

My idea had worked. Our second heads made us look normal to them. "I feel a lot safer now," I said.

I didn't have long to feel safe. Three creatures came tap-dancing at us, charging hard. "One-headers!" one of them shouted.

I gasped and felt my legs go weak. I leaned against the building to keep myself up. The two girls backed up with me.

"One-headers!" both of the creature's heads screamed.

He and his companions formed a line in front of us. Trapping us.

"Have you seen them?" he demanded. His four eyes moved from one of us to the other. His friends studied us in silence.

"Uh . . . seen them?" I stammered. My heart pounded so hard, my chest hurt.

His heads nodded. "They were spotted near here,"

he said. "Three or four one-headers. A whole bunch of them. Right on this street. Do you believe that?"

His friends muttered something to one another.

"Uh . . . no. I don't believe it," I choked out, still terrified that they were about to catch us.

"Keep an eye out for them," he said. "They couldn't have gone far."

The three of them started to dance past us.

I let out a long whoosh of air. I couldn't believe we had fooled them so completely.

I couldn't believe we were still safe.

"No problem," I said. "We'll keep watch for them." I raised two fingers to my forehead and gave the three of them a quick salute.

And then something horrible happened.

Something really horrible.

22

When I tapped my forehead in my two-fingered salute, I bumped the mannequin head. The head tilted to the side.

I tried to grab it. But the stick slid out from under my shirt collar.

I cried out as my head fell off and hit the sidewalk with a loud *craaack*, bouncing into the street.

The three creatures stopped dancing and uttered startled gasps. All twelve of their eyes were staring down at my head on the pavement.

"Uh . . . uh . . . I can explain!" I stuttered in a tiny voice.

One of them reached out and pulled Orly's fake head off her shoulders.

Cleo grabbed her mannequin head in both hands and held on to it.

"Looks like we found the one-headers," the group leader said. All of their heads were grinning now. Not happy grins—cold grins.

"We can't have you on the street," he said. "You'll frighten the children."

"Get moving. You're coming with us," one of his

friends ordered. They moved in on us, hooves clicking on the hard pavement.

"We . . . we're doomed," Cleo murmured, her voice trembling. She pulled off her mannequin head and tossed it. It bounced off the open capsule car, parked across from us.

Which gave me another idea.

I grabbed both girls by the arms. "Let's go. Hurry!"

I gave them a hard tug and burst toward the capsule car.

The startled creatures uttered angry cries and turned to chase us.

But it took only a few seconds to reach the low car and leap into the open top. Cleo and Orly dove in beside me. The roof slid closed above us. We were totally enclosed inside the capsule.

"We can escape in this," I said, struggling to catch my breath.

I heard the creatures' shouts outside the car.

"Just one problem," Cleo said, eyes wide with fright. "We don't know how to drive it."

I spun around and searched for the control panel. "Not a problem," I said. "How hard can it be?"

23

Outside, the shouts grew louder.

"Get out of there!"

"One-headers—you are caught! Come out *now*!"

"Get out! Get out! Get out!"

The angry creatures started to bang on the capsule. *Thud ... thud ...*

"We've got to *move*!" Orly yelled. "How do we start this thing up?"

"Uh ... well ..." I stared at the front of the car. Solid and smooth.

"Where are the controls?" Cleo cried, her voice cracking with fear. "Where is the steering wheel? How do you make it go?"

Thud ... thud ... thud ...

Angry shouts rang in from outside. "One-headers—come out!"

"You are caught. You cannot get away!"

"Give up now—before it's too late!"

Too late? What did THAT mean?

"The controls must be hidden," I said. Frantically, I began pressing the smooth metal front of the capsule. Nothing happened. No controls came into view.

I could see my reflection in the shiny metal.

Cleo and Orly began running their hands along the sides. Orly tapped the low roof.

Bang . . . bang . . . bang . . .

Fists pounded the sides of the capsule. The car began to rock from side to side.

"They're trying to turn us over!" Cleo shrieked.

"Where's the gas pedal?" Orly murmured to herself. "Where can it be? Where?"

She kicked at the floor and slapped her hands all over the sides of the car.

"Whoa! Wait!" I said. I spotted a tiny silver button cut into the curved metal front. "There it is! That has to be what we're looking for!"

My hand trembled as I stuck out my finger—and pressed the button as hard as I could.

I held my breath and waited for something to happen. Waited for the controls to pop into view. Waited for the car to move forward.

"Yes!" I cried out when I heard a low hum. "Yes!"

The hum grew louder.

"It's happening!" Orly cheered. "I think you did it!"

The hum grew even louder. We waited . . . waited . . .

And the capsule roof slid open.

Six hands reached for us.

We were caught.

SLAPPY HERE, EVERYONE.

Hahahaha. Murphy and his friends definitely need driving lessons!

They probably should have hailed a taxi!

I guess they learned a good lesson: It's very hard to escape in a PARKED CAR! Hahaha!

If you ask me, the three of them parked their *brains* back on Earth. That's the problem with having only one head. You're stuck with only one brain!

Are the three kids in major danger now?

Would this be a horror story if they *weren't*? Hahahaha.

24

Three creatures pulled us from the capsule car. They wore black pajamas, not white. Silver badges sparkled on their black caps.

"Don't try to escape," one growled. "We are Planetary Guards."

"What does that mean?" I asked.

"It means we are Planetary Guards," the biggest one shot back.

They lifted us from the roof of the car and dragged us through the crowd on the street. Everyone in the crowd had grown quiet. The creatures stared at us, wide-eyed, and oohed and aahed, as if they'd never seen anything like us before.

The three guards weren't rough, but, tap-dancing rapidly, they guided us quickly down the street. "Did you really think you could hide from us in that car?" one of them demanded.

"We weren't trying to hide," I answered. "We were trying to drive away."

"Well, why didn't you?" he asked.

"How do you drive it?" I asked. "We couldn't find the controls."

"Controls?" All six of their heads laughed. They rolled their eyes and laughed for a long time.

"There aren't any controls," the leader said finally. "You just tell it where you want to go."

So THAT's how they work. Their cars were a lot more advanced than ours.

"But what if you don't *know* where you want to go?" Orly asked.

"Then you get caught," the guard said. And the three of them laughed some more.

They pushed us up to their long black capsule car and helped us climb in through the roof. "Wh-where are you taking us?" I stammered.

"You'll see," came the reply.

"But—what are you going to do to us?" Cleo demanded. "What's going to happen?"

"You ask a lot of questions for someone with only one head," he replied.

"One-headers aren't allowed on Zoromisis 12," his other head told us.

"Why?" Orly asked. "Why aren't we allowed here?"

"Because you'll give the children nightmares" was the reply.

"We protect our children. We don't allow them to see monsters," another guard said.

"Monsters?" Orly cried. "We're not monsters!"

"Have you looked in a mirror?" the leader said. "You're monsters."

"We're just different from you," I argued.

"Yes, you are," the guard agreed. "You're monsters."

The car roof slid shut above our heads. It was

crowded in the capsule with the three of us and three big two-headed guards.

I felt beads of cold sweat on my forehead. My hands were suddenly cold and damp. A million questions flashed through my mind. None of them made me happy.

Where are they taking us? What do they plan to do to us?

I shut my eyes and silently wished Dr. Rayburne would come to our rescue—now. Would he be too late to save us?

I could feel the capsule sliding smoothly over the street. We were moving fast. Cleo had her eyes closed, her hands pressed to the sides of her face. Orly stared straight ahead, chewing her bottom lip. None of us said a word.

The ride seemed to go on forever. Finally, the capsule eased to a stop. The roof slid open. The pink sky had darkened to purple.

I stared up at a tall, dark building. All the buildings we had seen were round and low—mounds, shaped like the tops of snow cones. This building rose high in the sky. Built of black stone, it had a tower on each side and a wide, sloping roof. It looked like some kind of castle.

The three guards climbed out. Their hooves began tapping on the pavement. They turned, grabbed us under the shoulders, and lifted us from the car.

"Where are we?" I asked. "What is this building?"

The leader didn't answer. "Start dancing," he ordered. "You are about to meet our Supreme Leader."

"Huh? Supreme Leader?" I gasped.

Both of his heads nodded. "Prepare to meet Lord Hoofer, otherwise known as Hoofer the Horrible."

I gasped again. "Hoofer the Horrible? Why is he called Horrible?"

"You'll find out," the guard said.

The guards led us to a pair of shiny gold doors. The doors reached high up to the ceiling.

"Start dancing," the leader ordered.

"Dancing?" I said.

He nodded both heads. "You can't stand still in front of Hoofer the Horrible. You must dance in his presence."

"I . . . I'm not a very good dancer," Cleo said softly.

"Dance!" the guard boomed. "Dance! Everyone must dance! Don't you know the dance laws? Don't you know *anything*?"

His other head frowned at us. "Do you know the penalty for *not* dancing on this planet?"

"No. What is it?" I asked.

"The penalty is you have to see Hoofer the Horrible."

Was he making a joke?

I didn't think so.

Cleo, Orly, and I began moving our arms and legs, doing an awkward dance.

One of the guards laughed. "Your feet aren't built

for dancing," he said. He did a fast tap dance, raising his hooves high.

"Do your best," the guard leader said. "It won't be good enough to save your lives. But at least you'll know you gave it a good try."

I made a choking sound. "Save our lives?" I cried. "Save our lives?"

The guards swung the gold doors open and pushed us inside.

26

The three of us blinked in the bright pink light. Shrill noise that sounded more like screaming than music made me cover my ears.

I saw a band across the room, eight or ten crea-tures playing weird instruments. One musician banged on a drum set. But the drums were furry. They made a soft brushing sound. A horn was twisted up like a tuba, and water bubbled up from it as it played. One band member made *clock-clock-clock* noises by pounding on one of his heads.

The musicians all danced as they played.

The room was bigger than our gym at school. The ceilings were a mile high. The walls all glowed with pink light. Long purple drapes covered the floor-to-ceiling windows.

Small groups of dancers were tapping so hard, I could feel the floor shaking beneath my shoes. Their hooves drummed the floor, sending up a roar of thunder. They were all dressed in white. Their heads bobbed up and down in rhythm with their dancing.

The guards pushed us across the room, through

the groups of dancers. "Those are the Supreme Ruler's servants," the leader explained. "Awaiting their orders."

"They have to dance while they wait?" I said.

"Do you have any other stupid questions?" the guard snapped.

Orly pointed. "There's the throne," she said. A tall gold chair was raised on a purple platform. A group of servants were dancing around it, tapping their hooves and tossing their arms in the air.

Orly poked me in the side. "Keep dancing," she murmured.

I didn't realize I had stopped. I began moving my body and shuffling my feet again.

Where is Hoofer? I wondered.

And then I saw him. Through a line of dancers, I saw a two-headed creature on his back on the floor. He was kicking his legs in the air and spinning rapidly in a circle.

"It's like . . . break dancing," Cleo muttered.

Servants clapped and cheered him on as he spun on his back, bumping his heads on the floor in time with the band's rhythm. He wore purple pajamas, unlike everyone else in the huge chamber. And as we danced closer, I saw that he had purple flowers sprouting on top of both of his heads.

The guard gave me a push. "Go up to him and tell him how great he is. You don't want to insult him."

"Trust me," his second head chimed in, "you don't want to insult him. He needs to be told what an amazing dancer he is every few minutes."

"If no one tells him, he does his Unhappy Dance,"

the first head continued. "And you don't want to be around when he does his Unhappy Dance."

I kept swinging my arms and moving my knees. I couldn't stay in rhythm with the music because it just sounded like shrieking cats.

All the dancing made me feel out of breath. I pulled my inhaler from my pocket and gave it a few sprays. I kept dancing as I sprayed.

Finally, the band stopped playing. Two servants helped Hoofer the Horrible to his feet. He started to tap-dance to his throne—but he stopped when he spotted the three of us.

Both of his heads squinted at us. The flowers on his heads appeared to droop. "What are those ugly things?" he roared. He had a thunderous voice that rang off the high walls.

"One-headers, sire," the leader of the guards replied.

Hoofer covered all four of his eyes. "Sorry I had to see that," he said. "I'm about to have my lunch."

"We had to bring them in," the guard said. "Luckily, we caught them before they caused a panic."

Hoofer danced closer to us. "Were they littering?"

The guard nodded his heads. "Yes, they were littering, sire."

"No, we weren't!" Orly cried. "We weren't doing anything wrong. Just trying to get something to eat. And we definitely weren't littering!"

Both of Hoofer's heads scowled at her. "If you stand in the street with only one head, that's considered littering," he said.

My heart was pounding so hard in my chest, I could barely keep dancing. The two girls kept swaying from side to side and bending their knees. But I could see they were just as afraid as I was.

Hoofer suddenly raised his hands high in the air and shouted with both heads, "Leave us! Everyone—leave us! I will deal with the ugly ones!"

The floor rumbled as all the hooves turned and tap-danced out the door. It seemed to take forever for all the servants and band members and guards to leave the room.

Finally, the gold doors swung shut. The three of us were alone in the giant room with Hoofer the Horrible. He tap-danced to his throne and climbed onto it. He straightened his purple pajama sleeves, then raised his faces to us.

"Keep dancing," Orly whispered to me.

I was glad she kept reminding me. My legs were aching and my chest hurt. I was panting like a dog. But I didn't want to get into any more trouble than we already were.

Shuffle shuffle shuffle . . . slide.

The three of us danced in front of him.

We waited for Hoofer to speak. But he stared at us in silence, propping his chins on his hands.

Finally, I broke the silence. "Wh-what are you going to do to us?" I stuttered.

"Don't be so frightened," he said in his booming voice. "It will hurt, but it doesn't hurt for long."

27

Cleo let out a cry. I felt a wave of panic roll down my body. My legs suddenly felt rubbery and started to collapse. But I forced myself to keep dancing.

"The transplant will solve all our problems," Hoofer said.

"T-transplant?" Orly stuttered. "What kind of transplant?"

"A head transplant, of course," Hoofer said. A strange smile spread over both faces. "It's the best way."

Head transplant? The words echoed in my ears. I struggled to breathe. Without thinking, I grabbed for my inhaler. But it slipped from my trembling hand and bounced onto the floor.

I picked it up and shoved it back into my pocket.

"You will follow me to the Selection Room," Hoofer said. He climbed to his feet and danced away from the throne. "Let's not waste time."

"But—but—but—" I sputtered.

Cleo squeezed my hand. Her fingers were ice cold.

"You have to explain," Orly said. "You have to tell us what you're going to do."

"It should be obvious," the Supreme Ruler replied. "A head transplant is one of the simplest surgeries we have. First, you select a head . . ."

"Select a head?" I gasped.

"You select a head," Hoofer continued. "We build you a new neck. And then we transplant it onto your shoulders."

"Huh?" A gasp escaped my throat. Cleo squeezed my hand again. Orly was shaking her head no.

"Your second head takes about a week to connect with your body," Hoofer explained. "And then your one-head problem is solved forever. Once the new head starts to sprout flowers, you will be set free and can go about your lives. Monsters no more!"

"N-no, please—" I begged. "Please—"

Tap-dancing while he sat, Hoofer turned to Orly and smiled again. "I think we have the perfect new head for you. I'm pretty sure we have one that will match your old head." He brought one of his faces close to her. "What color eyes are those? I'm sure we can match them."

"Nooooo." Orly shook her head and wailed.

Hoofer waved a hand. "Follow me to the Selection Room. I think we have good head matches for all three of you."

"No—please—"

"Noooooo."

"We're begging you—"

The three of us began to plead.

"No. Don't thank me," he said. "I'm always ready to solve a problem."

A sob escaped Cleo's throat. Orly kept wailing

"Nooooo" and shaking her head. I struggled to breathe. I was too frightened to talk.

Hoofer danced to a door in the wall behind the throne. Then he turned and studied us one by one.

Then, to my surprise, he tossed back both of his heads and laughed. The twin laughter rose high and rang off the throne room walls. He laughed until tears rolled down all four of his cheeks.

Then he wiped his faces and said, "Just messing with you."

"Huh? Wh-what do you mean?" I choked out.

"Just messing with you," he repeated. "We don't know how to transplant heads. What a weird idea." He laughed again.

"But you said—" I started.

"Can't you take a joke?" he demanded. "We don't know how to transplant new heads." He studied Orly and Cleo. "But we can try sticking both of your heads on one body."

"NOOOO!" both girls screamed at once.

"Y-you can't do that!" I cried.

He turned his four eyes on me. "Oh, wait. We don't want to leave you out. Maybe we can stick your head on, too. A triple-header! Wow! I'm a genius!"

"Please, Hoofer! Please—!" Cleo begged.

"Listen to us, Hoofer," Orly started. "We—"

He raised a hand to silence her. "Let me be honest with you. I'm not Hoofer," he said. He let out another long laugh. "I'm not the Supreme Ruler. My name is Derek. I'm Hoofer's warm-up act."

"You're not Hoofer?" all three of us cried.

He shook his heads. "It's my job to get you ready

94

to see Hoofer. You know. Get you loosened up. Trust me, Hoofer is a lot more horrible than I am."

"You—you scared us to death!" I shouted.

He shrugged. "Just doing my job." Then he turned and pulled open the door in the wall. "Go on in," he said. "You can wait in there. Hoofer will be with you soon."

28

We stepped into the next room, and I gasped from the cold. I felt as if I'd stepped into a freezer.

Three guards stood just inside the door. "Hoofer likes to keep the room icy," one of them said. "Like his heart."

The room was dark, and I waited for my eyes to adjust to the dim light. It was as big as a ballroom and empty. Purple drapes lined all four walls. A golden throne stood at the far end of the room, a mile away.

"This is as close as we can come to the Supreme Ruler," another guard said. "You're on your own now."

"Good-bye," his other head added. "I don't suppose we will ever see you again."

That sent another hard shiver down my back. We watched the three guards exit through the door behind us.

All alone in the room, the three of us huddled together, shivering in the cold. I reached into my pajama pocket for the inhaler—and felt my fingers wrap around something else instead.

I pulled it out. The little rectangular black box. "Hey—!" I forgot I had tucked it away. I held it up. "Look. I found this in my jeans."

Orly took it from me and studied it closely. "It must be from Dr. Rayburne," she said. "This red button . . . It says *push here*."

A smile crossed my face. "We are saved!" I cried. "Don't you see what this is? This is what Rayburne gave us to return us home."

Cleo squinted at it. "Are you sure?"

"What else could it be?" I replied. "Wow. Perfect timing. We won't have to face Hoofer the Horrible after all!"

"Awesome! I knew Rayburne wouldn't leave us stranded here!" Orly said. "Push it, Murphy! Quick! Push it!"

"The door behind the throne—it's opening!" Cleo pointed at it. "Hurry. Push the button—now!"

"Home—here we come!" Orly shouted.

I gripped the black box tightly—and pressed the red button.

29

I shut my eyes and gritted my teeth and waited for the room to fade away. Waited for my molecules to dissolve and return me to Earth.

Waited.

I heard a click. Then a buzz.

Then a voice began to speak from the front of the box: "Greetings, travelers. This is Dr. Sidney Rayburne. Congratulations! If you are hearing my voice, it means that I have proven what an amazing genius I am! Thank you for helping me in your small way. Good luck to you—and happy travels!"

The box went silent.

I opened my eyes. I stared at the box. Silent now.

"Is . . . is that all?" Cleo stammered.

I shook the box. I lowered my thumb onto the button and pressed it again.

The same message played.

"Oh no," Cleo murmured, shaking her head sadly. "Oh no."

"I guess that's all," I muttered. "Just a stupid message." Angrily, I tossed the box to the floor.

The doors opened wider at the far end of the room.

A pink spotlight shone down on Hoofer the Horrible as he danced into the room at the front of a line of purple-dressed followers. He was much shorter than the creatures we had seen. And he appeared bone thin in his pink pajamas.

He wore gold crowns on his heads. And as I watched him do a furious, banging tap dance, I saw that his hooves were painted gold!

The music was fast and screechy. The followers bumped on their knees in rhythm to Hoofer's wild, noisy dance.

The three of us stood there shivering. Did Hoofer see us? Did he ever plan to stop dancing?

Finally, the music squealed to a stop. Dancing on their knees, the followers burst into applause. Hoofer took a deep bow. When he raised himself, his four eyes were locked on us.

The room grew silent except for the bumping of knees on the floor.

Hoofer studied us for a long time. Finally, he spoke, in a shrill squeaky voice. "Gumbo," he said. "Gumbo?"

At least, that's what I thought he said. It didn't make sense.

I could see he was waiting for us to reply. But we didn't know what to say. And I was shivering so hard, I bit my tongue!

"Gumbo," Hoofer repeated, a little louder. His eyes stared at us without blinking. He did a soft dance step as he waited, his gold hooves scraping the floor.

"You one-headers don't speak Gumbo?" he demanded.

All three of us shook our heads. "No, we don't," I choked out.

"What do you speak?" he asked.

"English," Orly answered.

"English doesn't exist," he snapped. "Are you lying to the Supreme Ruler?"

"I—I—I—" I stammered. "I'm speaking it. I'm speaking English."

"No, you're not," Hoofer insisted. "You can't. It doesn't exist. Ask anyone."

"But . . . we can't speak Gumbo!" Orly cried.

"Don't you go to school?" Hoofer demanded. He didn't give us a chance to answer. "Where did you come from?"

"We come from a planet called Earth," Orly told him.

"Earth doesn't exist," Hoofer said. "That's lie number twelve."

"No!" I cried. "It's number two!"

"The number two doesn't exist," he said. "That's lie trunteen." He danced closer. "How did you get here?" he pressed. "Remember not to lie."

"It—it's hard to explain," I said. "A scientist back home dissolved our molecules and sent them here. Then the molecules regrouped—and here we are."

"That's a ridiculous lie!" he shouted in his squeaky voice.

"Ridiculous!" the other head agreed.

"We don't have molecules on Zoromisis 12. Molecules are against the law here."

"Please. Believe us!" Cleo sputtered.

"Are you sure you don't speak Gumbo?" Hoofer

asked, squinting hard at us. "It might explain why you can never tell the truth."

"We—we just want to go home," I stammered.

"I don't think I can allow that," Hoofer replied. "You should have thought about how ugly you are before you traveled here."

"Then what are you going to *do* to us?" Cleo cried.

"Let me think about it . . . Okay, I've thought about it," Hoofer replied. "I've decided your fate. I don't think you're going to like it."

Hoofer tap-danced to the golden throne and sat down on it. He pointed to his hooves. "Gold me!" he shouted. "Gold me!"

A purple-pajamaed follower jumped up from his knees and hurried through a side door. He returned a few seconds later carrying a can in one hand and a brush in the other.

I quickly saw that the can held gold paint. The follower knelt at Hoofer's hooves and began splashing gold paint on them.

Hoofer moaned in pleasure. "That feels good," he said with a sigh. "The proper footwear makes all the difference."

"Thank you, sire," the follower said.

"Now paint your faces gold!" Hoofer shouted at him.

"Huh?" The follower gasped in surprise. "Paint my faces? Why?"

"That's your punishment for speaking to me without permission!"

The follower let out a whimper. Then he dipped

the paintbrush in the can and began splashing gold paint over his faces.

Hoofer returned his gaze to us. "I'm horrible, aren't I? It's my reputation. I have to live up to it."

He squinted at me with all four eyes. "You'd be disappointed if I wasn't horrible—wouldn't you?"

"Wh-what are you going to do with us?" I stammered.

"Well, I'll tell you one thing. I cannot let you leave my castle," he said. "That's for sure."

The words sent another shiver down my back. "Please, listen," I said. "If you let us go, we will return to our planet."

"And you will never have to see us again," Orly added.

Hoofer leaned back in the throne and kicked his hooves in the air. Gold paint splashed off them. A follower danced over to mop up the floor.

"I won't let you go," Hoofer said. "I don't believe you will go home. It's too nice here. Why would anyone leave?"

"You can let us out. We're not that scary!" Cleo cried.

Hoofer chuckled. "Have you looked in a mirror lately?"

I was so frightened, I stopped dancing. "Wh-what if we hide and stay out of sight?" I asked.

"I don't think so," Hoofer replied. "Now, dance! Dance!"

I groaned and began to sway and dip my knees again.

"All my people dance to show how happy they are!" Hoofer declared. "No one is allowed to be sad."

"I'm feeling pretty sad," I muttered.

"You *can't* feel sad if you dance," he said. He jumped to his feet and did a wild, frantic tap dance. "See how happy I am?"

"You . . . you want to keep us here forever?" Cleo choked out.

He nodded both heads. "Forever. What a happy word. Dance, everyone. Dance! How happy are we?"

"But—why?" I demanded. "Why not send us back to our planet?"

"Your planet doesn't exist," he replied, still dancing hard. "Our scientists tell us there is no life outside Zoromisis 12."

"But—but—" I started.

"Besides, what makes you think I know how to send you home? Do you think traveling from one planet to another is so easy?"

I didn't have an answer for that question. I stood staring at him, trembling and dancing at the same time.

"Stop fretting," he told us. "You will be my one-headed followers. You will remind me every day of how beautiful I am."

Tap-tap-tap.

He did a fast tap. Then a high cartwheel, his gold hooves reflecting the light. He came down for a perfect landing and kept dancing.

"You will spend your days," he said, "telling me what a great dancer I am."

Cleo let out a sob. I could see that Orly was also near tears.

If only Dr. Rayburne knew what horrible trouble we were in . . . maybe he would act fast to bring us home.

But . . . no.

"We are feeling very sad and upset," I told Hoofer in a tiny voice. "We are not happy."

"Of course you're happy," he said. "You're dancing, aren't you?"

I shook my head. I couldn't reply.

And then . . . I did something that changed everything.

31

My throat tightened, and I started to gasp for breath. My legs suddenly felt weak, about to collapse.

I reached into my pajamas pocket and tugged out the inhaler. I raised it to my face with a trembling hand. And squeezed it, sending a spray down my throat. Then I pushed it again for another spray.

But my hand was wet from sweat. The inhaler slipped, and the next two sprays floated into the air.

Still breathing hard, I saw Hoofer's eyes go wide. His mouths dropped open. "Aaaaaagh!" He uttered a cry and grabbed his two throats.

"What ... is ... that ... ?" he choked out in a hoarse whisper. He stopped dancing. "I ... I can't breathe!"

Gasps rang out all around. His followers stopped dancing, too.

Hoofer's eyes rolled in his heads. He squeezed his throats and made dry choking sounds. "Help me!" he moaned. "The invader—he *poisoned* me!"

I stood frozen, squeezing the inhaler in my fist, watching in horror.

Orly poked me in the ribs. "Spray some more!"

she cried. "Quick, Murphy—spray more! Maybe he'll let us go!"

I raised the inhaler to spray it again. But it fell from my hand and bounced across the floor.

Everyone dove for it at once. Two followers swiped at it, and it bounced from their hands. Another follower wrapped a hand around it. But Orly kicked his hand, and it flew into the air.

As the follower screamed in pain, I dropped to the floor and grabbed the inhaler. Before anyone could reach me, I raised it high and squeezed several spray mists into the air.

"Aaaaaagh!" Hoofer let out another wail. His heads were tossed back, mouths wide open. Horrible choking sounds erupted from his throats. It sounded like farm animals with their heads stuck in a fence.

Creatures were shouting angrily. I turned and saw a bunch of them lurching toward the three of us.

"Can't breathe . . . Can't breathe . . ." Hoofer wheezed. "Choking . . ."

"Spray more!" Orly shouted at me.

But before I could raise the inhaler, I felt strong hands wrap around my waist. One of the guards! I struggled to free myself, but I couldn't get loose.

Orly and Cleo screamed as guards tackled them from behind.

"Take them!" Hoofer gasped, wheezing and gagging. "Take them away!"

He squinted hard at us. "You want to see horrible? I'll show you horrible! No more Mister Nice Guy!" he boomed, choking and wheezing. "They must be *destroyed*!"

32

"Can we talk about this?" I said.

The guard tightened his grip on my shoulders and didn't reply.

In front of the throne, Hoofer was bent over as two followers pounded him on the back. "Can't breathe . . ." he moaned. "Can't breathe . . ."

"Let us go!" Orly cried. She jabbed the guard in the ribs with her elbow. But he didn't flinch or react at all.

The guards dragged us away from Hoofer, toward the front doors.

At the far end of the hall, Hoofer was choking and gagging and screaming. "Destroy them! Destroy them *now*!"

"You can't do this!" I shouted. "We're only kids!"

"What are kids?" Hoofer shrugged. "Kids don't exist on Zoromisis 12."

"You have to have kids!" I cried. "How can you have adults if you don't have kids?"

He didn't answer for a long moment. Then he said, "What are adults?"

Dancing hard, the guards pushed us from behind.

The doors slid open, and we were back in the long hall, pink walls glowing on both sides.

I had a desperate idea. What if I grabbed my inhaler and sprayed the guards? Would they start choking, too? Could we somehow break free and escape that way?

As if he could read my mind, the guard tightened his grip and pressed my arms against my sides. No way could I reach my pocket.

A frightened cry burst from my throat. "Are you really going to kill us?" I blurted out, my voice trembling.

"What part of *destroy* do you not understand?" he replied.

They shoved us into a dark doorway. Gray lights flashed on above us. Tall machines filled one wall, reaching to the high ceiling. Lines of red lights winked on and off. The machines hummed softly. The sound made the floor vibrate beneath our feet.

"Wh-what is this room?" I stammered.

"We call this the Good-Bye Room," the guard said.

My breath caught in my throat. They weren't kidding. This really was good-bye.

"Please—" Cleo started.

But a guard pulled her to the wall of machines. She started to struggle. But then she sighed. Her shoulders slumped. She lowered her head. She had given up.

A few seconds later, the three of us were chained to the machines. Hats shaped like metal domes were fastened to our heads. The domes were connected by many wires to the machines.

The machines began to hum louder. The floor actually shook. The vibrations pulsed through my body and made my head throb.

"By order of his Supreme Excellence," the guard leader said, "you must be dissolved."

"You—you're really going to dissolve us?" I stammered.

"Hoofer the Horrible didn't get his name by being a sweetheart," he replied.

"Please—please—" Cleo continued to beg.

"Don't do this!" Orly whimpered. "Please—"

"I—I—" I couldn't get any words out. My head was throbbing. My whole body pulsed and vibrated.

The leader moved to a control panel at the far side of the machine. He reached for a long black switch. "This will only take a second," he said.

"How can you do this?" Orly said, her voice breaking. "How can you kill us?"

The guard paused with his hand on the switch. "We're not going to kill you," he said. "We're just going to break your bodies down into particles of sand."

"But—" That's the only word I got out.

He pulled the switch.

33

I shut my eyes and clenched my jaw tight. And waited for the pain. Waited for the shock waves that would end my life.

Grains of sand.

I was about to dissolve into a pile of sand on the floor.

The roar of the machine rang in my ears. The dome helmet pulsed over my head.

I thought about my parents.

They'll never know that I ended up millions of miles away on a strange planet. They'll never know that a ruler named Hoofer the Horrible turned me into sand—all because I had only one head.

Orly and Cleo stood beside me, probably feeling the same terrifying vibrations that I felt. What were they thinking?

I never even got to say good-bye to them, I thought sadly.

The metal helmet crackled and hissed. I could feel it growing warmer. Would it keep getting hotter until it melted me?

I kept my eyes shut tight. I didn't want to see the

111

three of us dissolve into sand. The floor bounced under my feet. I struggled not to fall over.

A powerful vibration made me gasp. I wanted to reach up and rip the helmet off my head. But my hands were locked to the machine. I tugged with all my strength, but I couldn't budge them.

I'm dissolving, I thought.

I can feel myself fading away . . . coming apart . . . falling to pieces.

A loud crackle from inside the helmet—like a crack of lightning—made me scream.

And then . . . silence.

Silence.

I could hear my breaths, rapid wheezes of air.

The vibrations had stopped. The hum and roar of the machines had stopped.

I opened my eyes. And saw Orly beside me, eyes wide with shock. And Cleo beside her, tears tracking down the sides of her face.

I looked down and saw my shoes on the floor. My pajamas. My hands cuffed to the machine.

"I'm still here." The words burst from my mouth in a hoarse voice. "Whoa. We're still here."

Across the room, the guard with his hand on the switch turned to the other guards. "It didn't work," he told them. "Nothing happened."

"Now what?" his other head asked.

34

The guard let go of the switch and walked to the back of the machines. "Sometimes sand clogs up the works," he said. "Maybe we have to clean it out."

The other two guards disappeared behind the machines with him.

I tugged my arms. They slid out from the metal handcuffs that held them. With the power off, we were no longer attached.

"This is our chance," I whispered to Cleo and Orly. "Let's go!"

They pulled their hands free. Then all three of us ripped the metal caps off our heads. We spun away from the machines and took off.

The door slid open and we burst out into the long pink-lighted hall.

Which way? Which way?

"Where can we go?" Orly cried. "Where can we hide?"

"We're trapped here," Cleo said. "They'll find us no matter what. And if they don't find us, *then* what? We can't just close our eyes and wish ourselves back home!"

"We've got to try," I said. "Anything is better than being sand."

I heard the guards shouting in the lab next to us. And I heard their hooves thundering over the floor.

"They're coming after us. Quick!"

I took off running with the girls following close behind. At the end of the hall, we spun to the right—and ran into Hoofer and about a dozen of his dancing followers.

"Ohh!" I uttered a cry.

The followers filled the hall and blocked our path.

Hoofer covered his eyes with both hands. "Take them away," he ordered. "I'll never be able to *unsee* them. Never! Ohhh . . . so ugly . . . !"

The guards caught up to us. We were trapped between them and Hoofer's followers.

"We had trouble with the machine," the leader said. "But it's fixed now."

"Thank goodness," Hoofer said, tap-dancing hard, still covering his eyes. "Take them back and finish the job."

"Please—listen to us!" I cried. "Let me just say one final thing!"

What was I going to say?

I didn't know. I didn't have an idea in my head. I just wanted to stall for time.

"Let me just tell you something!" I cried. My brain whirred, desperately trying to think of something that might change Hoofer's mind.

He shook both heads. "No way," he said. "You've said enough."

He turned to the guards. "Report back when you

have dissolved them," Hoofer said. "And I'll throw a party to celebrate."

The guards grabbed us and, tap-dancing hard, dragged us back to the Good-Bye Room.

They cuffed our hands to the tall machine. Then they jammed the metal helmets over our heads.

I still tried to stall. "Could I just say a few last words?" I asked in a shaky voice.

"No," the guard answered.

He grabbed the switch and pulled it down.

This time, the machine worked.

SLAPPY HERE, EVERYONE.

Well . . . that's disappointing. I was hoping for a longer story!

What are we supposed to do now that the kids have been dissolved?

Maybe we should start tap-dancing, like everyone on Zoromisis 12. That will kill some time. Hahaha.

Know my favorite kind of dancing? It's break dancing. That's because I like to *break things* while I dance! Haha. Ooh, I'm evil. I'm so evil.

How did I get so evil? Practice! Hahaha.

Maybe Murphy and his friends can pull themselves together. Anyone out there have any Krazy Glue?

35

The light in the room dimmed. As the machine hummed and the vibrations pulsed through my body again, the colors faded. I stared into solid gray, as if a thick fog had lowered over us.

Black spots flickered in front of my eyes. The spots danced and flittered like dark moths. Then the spots grew bigger, like black balloons inflating. And I saw only black, darker than nighttime.

I opened my mouth to scream. But only a whisper escaped my throat.

Weak . . . I feel so totally weak . . .

My arms slumped at my sides. My knees started to fold. I could feel my legs go rubbery. I struggled to breathe.

And then I disappeared.

Just faded away. Was I floating now? I felt so light, light as a feather. I couldn't feel anything beneath my feet. I couldn't feel anything.

How long did I float in the blackness?

I didn't know. I fell asleep. No. It was more than sleep. I wasn't there at all. I just wasn't there.

My last thought was of Orly and Cleo. Were they as frightened as I was?

That was the last question I asked. And then I was gone. I wasn't anywhere. I didn't exist.

"Huh? What—?"

I heard my voice before I saw anything. Yes. It was definitely me.

I blinked my eyes. I had eyes!

The darkness faded and light seemed to spread all around me.

"Hello?" Confused, I tested my voice. "It's me. Murphy. Where am I?"

I shook my head. I had a head! I tapped my shoes on the floor.

Yes! It was me! Back together again.

And beside me stood Orly. And beside her, Cleo. Looking just as surprised and confused as I was.

We were still wearing the headphones we had on when we left Earth. Rayburne's machine must have duplicated our bodies in space. I reached up to my ears and pulled the headphones off.

Cleo and Orly were blinking and smiling and testing their arms and legs. They pulled their headphones off, too, and let them dangle to the floor.

"Where are we?" Orly cried.

And as she asked the question, I recognized the two men staring at us from across the room. I stepped away from the machine I'd been hooked up to. My legs were shaky, but I could walk.

"We—we're back!" I stammered.

Dr. Rayburne and Mr. Hawkins, our teacher, had smiles on their faces.

"Welcome home," Rayburne said. He swept a hand through his straight white hair. "I imagine you've had quite a journey."

What had happened? My guess? The machine on Zoromisis 12 broke up our molecules and sent them right back to where they came from. We traveled here just the way we had traveled to the other planet.

Mr. Hawkins rushed forward and hugged all three of us at once. "Thank goodness!" he cried. "I was so worried about you!"

"We're safe! We're safe!" Cleo and Orly jumped up and down, cheering.

"How do you feel?" Rayburne asked, studying us.

"A little shaky," I said. "But not bad."

Cleo turned to our teacher. "You—you left without us!" she said to him.

"I—I know," Hawkins stammered. "It was an emergency. I left in a panic. I'm so sorry. As soon as I discovered you three weren't on the bus, I hurried back for you. Tell me—how are you?"

"They're fine," Rayburne interrupted. "Perfectly fine."

His eyes went from me to Orly to Cleo. "Tell me the important thing," he said. "Did it work? Did my brilliant invention work? Am I a genius? Tell me— did I send you to Zoromisis 12?"

I stared back at him, thinking hard.

"Well?" he demanded. "Answer!"

"No," I said. "It didn't work. I fell asleep and nothing happened."

119

36

Cleo gasped. Orly blinked several times, then stared hard at me.

I tried to signal them with my eyes. I wanted them to figure out why I was lying to Dr. Rayburne.

The scientist sputtered and tugged at his mustache. "But—but—surely the transition machine sent you to the other planet."

"I didn't go anywhere," I replied. "And neither did they. I fell asleep and then I woke up right back here in your lab."

"Im-impossible!" Rayburne stuttered.

"I had a nice sleep," Orly said. "I dreamed about my little sister. We were eating ice cream."

Orly got it! She understood what I was doing!

I wanted Rayburne to think his machine was a failure. That way, he wouldn't force anyone else to travel into space.

"I didn't have any dreams," Cleo said. "But I had a nice, peaceful sleep."

"Maybe you've invented a sleep machine," I told Rayburne.

"No!" he cried. "Noooo! A failure!" He slumped into a chair and buried his face in his hands.

Mr. Hawkins motioned us to the door. "Let's go," he said. "I need to call your parents. They've been very worried."

We stepped outside. I gazed up at the sky. The sun was yellow—not pink.

We really were home.

The three of us didn't say a word about our space travel to Mr. Hawkins. We were quiet all the way to our homes. Hawkins kept apologizing and apologizing for stranding us in the observatory. "We left in such a rush. But I should have taken attendance on the bus. My bad!" he said. "You three must have been very frightened."

"Us? Frightened?" Orly said. "No way."

"What was there to be frightened about?" Cleo said.

"We knew you'd come back for us," I said.

"Rayburne is a brilliant scientist," Hawkins said. "But I think he's a little weird."

"A little," I agreed.

Mom and Dad greeted me with hugs. "We can't wait to hear about your adventures in the observatory," Mom said.

"Maybe at dinner," I said. "I'm a little zoned out from all the excitement."

"Did you get any ideas for how to end your story about going to Mars?"

"Lots of ideas," I told her. "*Too many* ideas!"

I was never so happy to be back in my room. Normal life!

I sat down on the edge of my bed and gazed around the room at my posters of the universe. On my dresser, I had two photographs signed by real astronauts. A model of our solar system dangled from the ceiling.

Hey, I'm an astronaut, too, I told myself. I traveled a lot farther in space than any real astronaut. Thinking about it made me start to feel excited again. A little out of breath.

Relax, Murphy, I told myself. *Everything is normal again. And you're really lucky. Your molecules were scrambled twice, and nothing bad happened. Everything turned out fine.*

"Totally fine," I said out loud. "I'm totally fine."

I reached into my pocket and pulled out my inhaler. I raised it to my face and sent a couple of sprays down my throat.

I was about to put it away when I heard a voice.

"Hey—what about me? Send a few sprays my way!"

"Huh? Who said that?" I looked around my room, but there was no one there.

"Well, I'm waiting," the voice said.

"Where are you?" I spun around. And caught my reflection in the mirror. And saw a new head growing right beside my old one.

"Oh noooo," I moaned. *"Not* totally fine!"

EPILOGUE FROM SLAPPY

Hahaha. Looks like Murphy has a new friend! Hope they get along! Hope they don't fight over who gets the last slice of pizza! Haha.

I know what to buy Murphy for his birthday. New shirts! Hahaha. Where do you buy shirts with *two* collars? He may have to go back to Zoromisis 12 to get dressed!

Makes me think of the old saying: Two heads are better than one. It's so nice that Murphy will never be home alone again! Hahaha.

I'd like to take Murphy to a baseball game. Know why? I *love* double-headers! Hahaha.

Well . . . let's say "good-bye good-bye" to Murphy. There are lots of other scary stories to tell.

I'll see you soon with another *Goosebumps SlappyWorld* book.

Remember, this is *SlappyWorld*.

You only *scream* in it!

DON'T BE SCARED, IT'S A SLAPPY SPECIAL EDITION!

This special edition reveals the untold true story behind the world's most dreadful dummy.
Turn the page for a spine-tingling sneak peek—if you dare!

Where did Slappy come from? What brought him to life?

There are many stories and legends about Slappy's origin.

Some say that an evil magician carved him out of wood from a haunted coffin. One story goes that he escaped from a puppet factory in Cincinnati. Another legend says that the ghost of a ten-year-old boy lives inside Slappy's head.

I'm not sure about those stories. I think the story I'm about to tell you is the true one.

Slappy's story starts two hundred years ago in a tiny village in Europe. So let's head there—to a cottage at the edge of the deep woods. That's where you will meet Darkwell the puppet maker. He is also a magician.

Darkwell is going to cast a secret spell. A spell that will change many lives as it travels through the centuries.

What is this mysterious spell?

What is this curse that's been kept secret for two hundred years?

Be patient, readers. Let me tell you the story . . .

Flames crackled in the fireplace. They sent shadows leaping and dancing over the walls of the small cottage. Outside, the wind moaned, shaking the glass in the window and whistling through the cracks in the thin walls.

Feeling a chill, Ephraim Darkwell pulled his gray robe tighter around him. His hood fell over his forehead, covering the old man's long white hair. He leaned over his workbench, his hand moving a knife quickly, smoothly.

Darkwell's dark eyes locked on the rounded piece of wood he was sculpting. A head. He rubbed his thumb over its scalp, brushing away a splinter. He worked the slender wooden eyelids up and down.

The face was nearly completed. Darkwell knew he had little time to finish. He knew the rumors. The talk in the village. He had explained to everyone that he was a simple dollmaker, a builder of puppets.

But the superstitious villagers didn't believe him. They spied on him. From the woods behind the cottage, they watched him through the cottage's only window. Somehow, they learned the truth.

Darkwell was no simple puppet maker. He was a sorcerer who could magically bring his puppets to life. A master of the dark arts. But he had vowed never to use his power for evil.

He came to the village to work in peace. He wanted to be left alone to build his creations and explore the magic he had learned. He meant the villagers no harm . . .

Until yesterday . . . when Darius Koben, the chief constable, burst into the cottage, red-faced and wheezing with anger. In that moment, Darkwell knew his peace had ended.

"You and your nephew must leave," Koben boomed, banging his cane against the floor with each word. "You are not wanted here. Your evil magic has frightened everyone."

Darkwell bowed his head. "I am a simple doll-maker," he insisted.

Koben smacked the cane hard against the wooden wall. His cheeks reddened above his gray beard.

"Your lies cannot protect you, Darkwell," he shouted. "You have been seen talking to your dolls— and they have been seen talking back. They move about your cottage as if they are alive. You cannot deny the truth. It is too late!"

"I mean no harm," Darkwell insisted.

"I did not come to argue," the constable said, waving the cane in the air. "I came to warn you."

"Warn me?"

"There is talk in the village," Koben said, lowering his voice. "There is talk of burning you out. The torches are already lit, Darkwell. Do you understand? Their anger—it cannot be controlled."

Darkwell stared at the constable, allowing his words to sink in.

"Get out!" Koben shouted. "Leave now! You and your nephew. Pack up and get out if you value your lives!"

The constable spun on his cane and stomped from the cottage. The slender door banged in the swirling wind. Darkwell pulled the door closed, feeling the cold air on his face.

He shivered, but not from the cold. He shivered in anger that his work must be interrupted. He was about to finish his most magical creation yet. He couldn't allow the foolish, ignorant villagers to destroy his best work.

Darkwell leaned over the workbench all night, his hands working feverishly. And now he held the doll in front of him.

"The fools will be sorry," he told the doll. "They have pushed me too far. Once you are finished, we will make them sorry they are alive."

The lifeless eyes gazed up at him. The wooden lips turned up in a grin. The head lay tilted to one side.

"Almost complete, my little friend," Darkwell said. But then he uttered a startled gasp as the cottage door swung open.

A figure staggered in. His hair flew wildly about his face. His white shirt was stained, one sleeve nearly ripped off. A trickle of blood ran from his nose. His cheek was cut, dark blood forming a crooked line.

"Isaac!" Darkwell cried, staring in horror at his twelve-year-old nephew. "Isaac! What have they done to you?"

"Th-they beat me, Uncle," the boy stammered.

Darkwell swept his arms around him and guided him to a wooden chair. He brought a wet cloth from the pot beside the hearth and dabbed at the blood on his nephew's face.

"Who did this, Isaac?" Darkwell demanded. "Tell me the whole story."

"I . . . I went to buy the supplies you wanted," the boy began slowly. He smoothed down the sides of his coppery hair with both hands. "But they stopped me outside the village store."

"Who?" Darkwell asked gently. "Who stopped you?"

"They said you weren't fit to bring me up," Isaac said, ignoring the question. "They said they could not leave me with someone so evil. They—they are going to take me, Uncle. Take me away."

Darkwell placed a hand on his nephew's trembling shoulder. "I won't let them," he murmured in the boy's ear. "You do not need to worry."

"I . . . I tried to tell them you were good. I said

you were kind. I said you wouldn't harm anyone. That's when . . ."

Isaac's words caught in his throat.

"That's when they beat you?" Darkwell demanded.

Isaac nodded. "I stuck up for you, and it made them angry. I tried to get away. But some boys grabbed me. They said their fathers were coming for us—with torches. Coming to burn us out."

"Don't worry, my boy." Darkwell patted his nephew's head. "You do not have any reason to fear. I will make sure of it."

He helped Isaac to his feet and led him to his cot against the wall. "Lie down. Sleep now. Sleep and dream of good things."

Isaac obediently lowered himself to the cot and curled onto one side. "Good night, Uncle."

Darkwell stood watch until his nephew fell asleep. Then, shaking his head, he strode back to the workbench. He lifted the doll he had been crafting and brushed some wood chips off its chest.

"Your time has come," he said. He reached for the clothing he had sewn for the doll. He pulled the trousers over the legs, then worked the arms into the shirt and then the jacket.

"You will not disappoint me," Darkwell told it. "I have completed you just in time. When the villagers arrive to destroy me, you will be ready."

The doll stared back at him with glassy eyes. Its grin was frozen on its face. It sat hunched over on the worktable.

Darkwell propped it up so that its back leaned

straight against the wall. He raised the head so that its eyes looked into his eyes.

"Yes! Yes! My heart is pounding!" Darkwell declared. "I have learned much magic and accomplished many things. But it has all been leading up to you!"

The sorcerer took a step back from the work table. He cleared his throat loudly. His eyes on the doll, he took a deep breath—and shouted these words to the ceiling:

"*Karru Marri Odonna Loma Molonu Karrano!*"

3

Darkwell's hands trembled as he gazed at the doll. He tucked them under his robe and held his breath. The words he had just spoken rang in his ears.

The only sounds in the cottage were the crackling of the fire and the soft breathing of Isaac, asleep on his cot.

Darkwell stood frozen in place, waiting for the magic to take hold. And then it happened. The doll's eyes blinked once. Twice. The mouth closed slowly with a soft *click*.

"Yes," the sorcerer whispered. "Yes. It is working. You are alive." The old man took a deep breath and forced his heart to stop racing in his chest.

The doll blinked once more and turned its wooden head from side to side, as if testing it. The painted lips moved up and down, making a soft *click* each time.

"Speak!" the sorcerer commanded.

The doll raised a wooden hand and touched the side of its face. It blinked a few more times, moving its head up and down. And then a soft, harsh voice rattled from somewhere inside it: "Where am I?"

Darkwell uttered a cry. "Yes! Yes! You can speak!"

"Where am I?" the doll repeated. And then, in the same raspy voice, only stronger this time: "Who are you? Who am I?"

The old sorcerer hugged himself as if to hold in his excitement. "We have no time for questions," he told the doll. "They are coming to destroy me. But you are here now. You were created to carry out my evil when I am gone."

The doll blinked. Its mouth dropped open. "Evil? Tell me . . . why am I evil?"

"You are my revenge," Darkwell replied. "My revenge on those fools who do not understand how brilliant I am . . . the fools who would destroy me. If they succeed, I am about to perish—"

"Perish?" the doll repeated.

"But my evil will live on through you," Darkwell continued. "I have cast a powerful spell. I have spoken powerful words to bring you to life. Listen to me carefully. I won't have time to explain it again."

The dummy lowered its hands to the workbench and leaned toward the sorcerer. "I am listening."

"From now on," Darkwell said, "when the secret words are spoken, you will awaken and perform the evil you were created for."

"What does that mean?" the doll demanded. "What should I do?"

"You will terrify people," Darkwell replied. "You will scare them to death. You will make people scream in fright and cry. And you will make them your servants for life."

"For life," the doll repeated.

"I have given you a cute name," the sorcerer said. "So that people will not suspect your true nature. Your name is Slappy. A name fit for a circus clown. But you are no clown. Instead of bringing laughter into the world, you will bring screams of horror."

"Hahahaha!" Slappy tilted back his head and uttered a shrill laugh. "Screams of horror. Father, that sounds like fun!"

Darkwell started to speak but stopped. He heard voices in the distance. Through the small front window, he saw yellow light flickering against the black night sky.

Torchlight? Were the villagers approaching?

Darkwell fought back the feeling of panic in his chest. "There is more I need to tell you, Slappy," he said, his eyes on the window. "I must give you a warning."

Slappy blinked. "A warning, Father?"

The sorcerer nodded. "The spell I have cast gives you great mind-control powers. But beware of its one weakness."

Behind Darkwell, Isaac stirred in his cot. Eyes still closed, he stretched his hands above his head. "Is it morning, Uncle?" he called.

Darkwell ignored him. "Here is my warning, Slappy. You must do something evil *every day* that you are awake. If you are awake for a day and fail to terrify someone, the spell will end—and you will sleep forever!"

"Hahaha!" The doll uttered its cold laugh once again. "This sounds like interesting work," he rasped. "I will obey you, Father. I will be evil every day that I am awake."

"You have no choice, Slappy," Darkwell replied. "If you fail to scare someone every day, you will sleep forever. *And no words will be able to wake you!*"

"Uncle?" Isaac sat up on his cot.

At the same moment, a sharp *thud* at the cottage door made the boy cry out.

Another hard *thud*. The sound of an axe chopping at the wood.

Darkwell grabbed Slappy in both hands and pressed him against the front of his robe. "The villagers!" he exclaimed. "They have come for us!"

Bright yellow torchlight flamed outside the cottage window. Angry shouts nearly drowned out the *thud*s of the chopping axes.

Isaac ran to Darkwell and tugged at the old man's robe. "Help, Uncle. What shall we do? You promised—"

"I promised you will not have to worry about them," Darkwell said. He hugged Slappy to his chest, his dark eyes wide, fixed on the door. "I keep my promises, Isaac."

A deafening crash followed the *crack* of splintering wood. The door crumbled as it fell open. Heavy boots stomped over it as men in dark clothing and black hoods burst into the cottage.

Torch flames licked at the low ceiling. The voices of the men were loud and angry.

Darkwell slid Slappy to a corner of the workbench. Then he turned to face the intruders.

Chief Constable Koben pushed his way to the front, swinging his cane to scatter the men from his path. His face flamed red in the bright torchlight.

He raised the cane and pointed it at Darkwell. "You did not heed my warning, old man!" he boomed.

Behind him, the hooded villagers uttered angry words and jabbed their torches menacingly toward the sorcerer and his nephew. Isaac clung to his uncle's robe. Whimpering cries escaped his throat.

"You have no reason to invade my home and threaten me," Darkwell said, shouting over the murmurs of the men. He set Slappy down on the worktable and placed his hands on Isaac's shoulders. "I am a simple dollmaker."

"We did not come for a discussion," Koben shouted. "We know what you are, and we will not have you in our village. We are decent people, and we obey the laws of nature—not the laws of darkness!"

"Burn the house! Burn the house!" some men began to chant. "Burn it down! Burn it all!"

Koben raised his cane to silence them. "Darkwell, we have come to put an end to your evil!" he boomed.

"Burn it down! Burn it down!" The flames appeared to grow brighter as the men stabbed their torches toward the ceiling.

Koben struck his cane against the floor. "Silence! We will burn it down—and this old sorcerer with it. But first we must deal with the boy."

"Noooo!" Isaac wailed. He held on tightly to the front of Darkwell's robe.

Koben took a few heavy steps across the room. "We are taking the boy," he said. "Hand him over to us. Your days are over, Darkwell. Your doom is today. But the boy will be saved. We are taking him from you now."

"Uncle, please—" Isaac cried. "You promised!"

Koben stretched out both hands. "Hand him over, Darkwell. Hand him over *now*!"

A stillness fell as Darkwell stared back at the chief constable with his icy gray eyes. After a long moment, the old sorcerer broke the silence.

"Okay," he said. "Here he is. You can take him."

"Nooooo!" Isaac wailed.

Darkwell grabbed the boy's wrists and pushed him toward the chief constable. "He's all yours," Darkwell said.

Koben blinked in surprise. He took Isaac around the waist.

Isaac cried out again—and struggled free. He dove back to Darkwell and clung to the front of the sorcerer's robe. "Noooo! Please! Noooo!"

The hooded men looked on in stunned silence. Their low murmurs stopped. The torches in their hands locked in place.

"The boy is yours," Darkwell said again. He shoved Isaac toward Koben.

Koben gripped Isaac again. He started to pull him to the door.

"Wait," Darkwell said. "Please. May I have a minute to say good-bye to him?"

Darkwell reached under his robe. He pulled out a large metal key. He stepped up to Isaac and swept up the back of the boy's thick hair.

Koben's eyes went wide as Darkwell pushed the

key into the back of Isaac's head. Everyone heard a *click* as the sorcerer turned the key.

Isaac's eyes closed. His mouth fell open. His knees collapsed. He dropped to the floor.

Koben uttered a horrified shout as Isaac's head hit the floor and split in two. It cracked open like a coconut shell. Gasps rose throughout the cottage as everyone stared at the wires and tubes inside the head.

Darkwell tucked the key under his robe. "I promised Isaac he wouldn't have to worry about you," he said.

Koben took a few staggering steps back until he bumped into the startled men. "The boy—he . . . he isn't real!" Koben stammered, pointing his cane at the body on the floor. "He is one of your creations!"

A thin smile crossed Darkwell's face. "One of my best," he said.

"Burn him! Burn him *now*!" a man shouted.

And the others took up the chant. "Burn him! Burn him! Burn him!"

Swinging their torches, they stormed forward. Darkwell raised both hands as if to shield himself.

The ceiling caught fire. A chair and Isaac's cot burst into flame. Then, with a crackling explosion, the workbench began to burn.

About the Author

R.L. Stine says he gets to scare people all over the world. So far, his books have sold more than 400 million copies, making him one of the most popular children's authors in history. The Goosebumps series has more than 150 titles and has inspired a TV series and two motion pictures. R.L. himself is a character in the movies! He has also written the teen series Fear Street, and the Mostly Ghostly and Nightmare Room series. He is currently writing a series of graphic novels entitled Just Beyond. R.L. Stine lives in New York City with his wife, Jane, an editor and publisher. You can learn more about him at rlstine.com.

Catch the MOST WANTED Goosebumps® villains UNDEAD OR ALIVE!

SPECIAL EDITIONS

scholastic.com/goosebumps

GBMW42

CONTINUE THE FRIGHT AT THE GOOSEBUMPS SITE
scholastic.com/goosebumps

FANS OF GOOSEBUMPS CAN:

- PLAY THE GHOULISH GAME:
  GOOSEBUMPS: SLAPPY'S DROP DEAD HOUSE

- LEARN ABOUT NEW BOOKS AND TERRIFYING CLASSICS

- TAKE A QUIZ AND LEARN WHICH TYPE OF MONSTER YOU ARE!

- LEARN ABOUT THE AUTHOR WHO STARTED IT ALL: R.L. STINE

■ SCHOLASTIC

HOME BASE

THE Goosebumps SERIES COMES TO LIFE IN A BRAND-NEW DIGITAL WORLD

MEET Slappy—and explore the Goosebumps Zone.
PLAY games, create an avatar, and chat with other fans.

Start your adventure today! Download the **HOME BASE** app and scan this image to unlock exclusive rewards!

SCHOLASTIC.COM/HOMEBASE

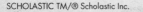

Goosebumps SlappyWorld

THIS IS SLAPPY'S WORLD—
YOU ONLY SCREAM IN IT!